P9-CDI-054
DISCARD

LEGENDS OF
LOTUS ISLAND
THE GUARDIAN TEST

LEGENDS OF LOTUS ISLAND

THE GUARDIAN TEST

BY CHRISTINA SOONTORNVAT

ILLUSTRATED BY KEVIN HONG

Scholastic Press / New York

Library of Congress Cataloging-in-Publication Data available

ISBN 978-1-338-75915-0

10 9 8 7 6 5 4 3 2 1 23 24 25 26 27
Printed in Italy 183

First edition, March 2023
Book design by Cassy Price

For Elowyn and Aven—this story
started with you

SANTIPAP
ISLANDS
NAKHON
ISLAND
THE SANTIPAP SEA
BIDIBOP
ISLAND
BIG CRAB
ISLAND
TORTOISE NOSE
ISLAND
SMALL
CRAB
ISLAND
SOM
ISLAND
LITTLE
ISLAND

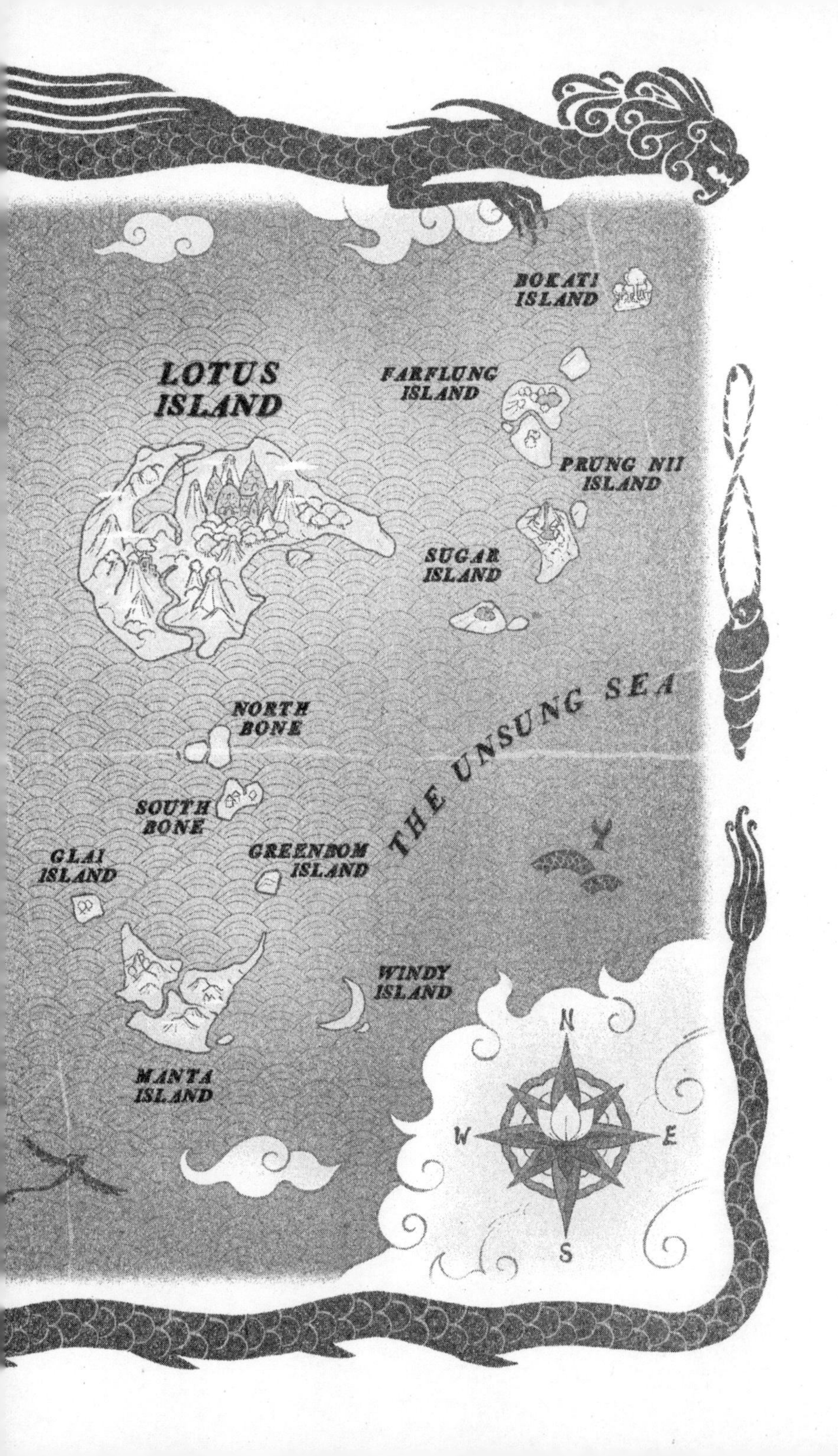
BOKATI ISLAND
LOTUS ISLAND
FARFLUNG ISLAND
PRUNG NII ISLAND
SUGAR ISLAND
THE UNSUNG SEA
NORTH BONE
SOUTH BONE
GLAI ISLAND
GREENBOM ISLAND
WINDY ISLAND
MANTA ISLAND
N
W
E
S

Worms always think they know everything.

"Come on, friends, not there by the squash. You want to be over here by these chai-melons, trust me." I scooped the worms out of the dark, fluffy soil and set them down near the chai-melon vine. "There. Now make that dirt good and soft, because I want to eat some big, fat melons this summer."

I stood up and walked around our garden. The eggplant and crisp-cumbers were doing great this year. And of course our chili plants and snake beans were growing wild, as always. But my main concern was our fruit trees. This year I was determined that we would have *everything*: jackfruit, mangoes, tea fruit, rose apples, even stinky durian.

I heard a rustling in the mango leaves. "Oh, sorry to wake you," I whispered to the family of fox bats that hung upside down, sleeping. "Now, don't forget what we agreed. You get the mangoes up top and leave the low stuff for us, okay?"

The mama fox bat yawned and shut her eyes again. A couple of years ago they nibbled bites out of every mango on our tree. But now that I'd convinced Grandpa to take down the nets, they only took the fruit that was too high for us to reach.

In a couple of weeks it would all start getting ripe. I could practically taste the feast in my mouth. The only fruit we could never seem to grow was—

"Plum!"

I turned around to see Grandma shuffling down the hill toward me. "Over here in the orchard, Grandma!"

"Plum," she huffed, "come on up to the house, dear."

"Is everything okay?"

"Of course it is!" she said, but I saw the corner of her mouth twitch. She always did that when she wasn't telling me the whole story.

I wondered what was going on, but I knew better than to pester her.

I let her lean on my shoulder as we walked slowly back up the hill to our house. The cool evening breeze felt so good after a long, sweaty day working in the garden. As always, we paused in the one spot where we could see the entire island. Our little wooden house and barn stood at the top of the hill. The garden and orchard were down below, near the freshwater spring. On the other side, Grandpa's rice fields sloped down to the coconut grove. And all around, the blue ocean sparkled.

The sun was starting to set. The fox bats were waking up, and the swallows were already swooping overhead. I imagined them calling out to us: *Day is done! Day is done! Time for night!*

"Good night!" I called up to them. "Don't forget our deal about the mangoes!"

Out on the water, I spotted the little blue postal boat zipping back toward Big Crab Island. My stomach did a flip. We almost never got mail. I glanced at Grandma for some hint as to what was going on, but her face was like a stone.

Before we got to the house, Grandma patted my hand. "Oh, and tomorrow, remind me that I need your help with the wheelbarrow. The chai-melon bed is full of rocks, and we've got to move them so the worms can get in."

I looked back at the garden and shook my head. Those worms were never going to let me hear the end of this.

CHAPTER 2

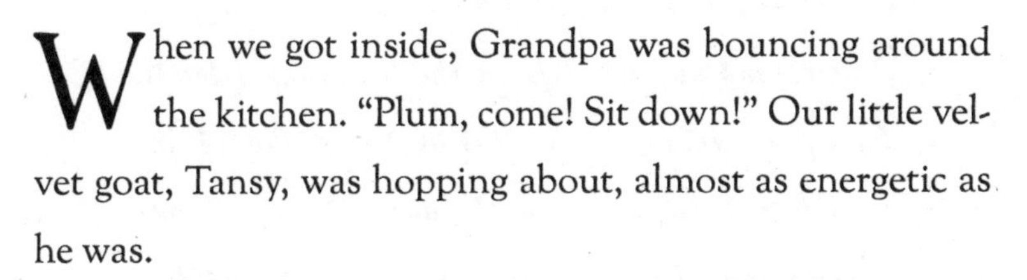

When we got inside, Grandpa was bouncing around the kitchen. "Plum, come! Sit down!" Our little velvet goat, Tansy, was hopping about, almost as energetic as he was.

He pulled out a chair for me and poured himself a cup of tea, sloshing it onto the table.

Tansy clip-clopped over and put her soft head in my lap. "Grandpa, what's going on? Why are you so excited?"

Grandma sighed and went to the stove to stir the soup. Her face looked like she'd sucked on a bitter lemon.

Grandpa patted my knee. "Plum, you know how we've talked about you spending more time around other people?"

"Yes," I said, still confused. "Is this about that summer camp on Big Crab Island?"

Grandma clanged her spoon against the pot. "Just tell her already."

Grandpa reached inside his jacket pocket and brought out an envelope. "Read it for yourself, my dear."

> *Dear Miss Plum,*
>
> *I have the pleasure of inviting you to the Guardian Academy on Lotus Island. For centuries, the Guardians have fulfilled their ancient duty to protect and nurture life in the Santipap Islands. Every ten years, a new class of Novice Guardians is selected to train with our Masters. Your application identified you as a strong candidate to join the next Novice class. Please arrive on the full moon to begin the first phase of your training.*
>
> *Sincerely,*
>
> *Master Sunback*

My mind tumbled around in a confused mess.

Tansy started nibbling the paper. "Stop that!" I jerked it

out of her mouth. "Grandpa, this must be a mistake. I didn't apply to the Guardian Academy."

He grinned. "I applied for you."

I sat straight up. "What! And you didn't tell me?"

"I didn't think you'd get in!" He cleared his throat. "What I mean is . . . I didn't want you to get your hopes up in case it didn't work out."

"But I . . . I can't be a Guardian. Those people are *magical.* They travel all over the islands doing . . . I don't know, magical stuff!"

Grandpa waved his fingers at me. "They all started off as regular kids."

"They transform into spectacular creatures," I said. "Like hywolves and zorahawks and—"

"Gillybears," offered Grandma.

I threw my hands up. "And gillybears! Can you imagine me as a gigantic white bear diving into the waves? It's ridiculous!"

"That's what the Academy is for—to learn." Grandpa leaned over to take my hand. "Plum, your Grandma and I have been talking about this for some time. You are such a special girl, and that is becoming clearer the older you get. You have such a way with plants and animals. You talked to those fox bats, and now we finally get to our enjoy our mangoes."

I rolled my eyes. "It's not like they *actually* understood me."

"Well, you can't spend your whole life here, being a farmer on this little island. You are meant to do great things. I know it!"

I looked at Grandma, but she had turned her back to me.

So they had been talking about me in secret? It would have been nice if they had let me in on this decision. I folded my hands in my lap. "Thank you, Grandpa, but I don't want to go," I said quietly.

"Plum, don't be silly. Think of the opportunity—"

"I'm not going!" I stood up. "Grandpa, if I'm gone, who will take care of the garden? Who'll take care of Tansy? Who will—"

Take care of you? I thought.

Grandma set the soup pot down on the table with a loud clatter. "Dinner's ready."

Tears welled up in my eyes. How could they expect me to eat when they had just turned my whole world upside down?

"I'm not hungry!" I yelled. I bolted out the door and into the night.

CHAPTER 3

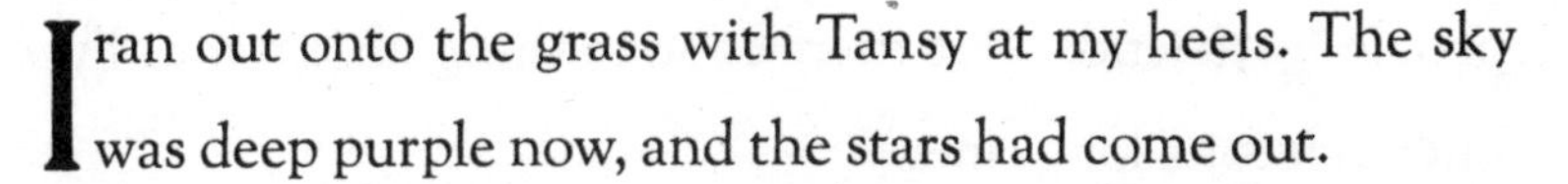

I ran out onto the grass with Tansy at my heels. The sky was deep purple now, and the stars had come out.

I wiped my cheeks and dribbling nose. Tansy put her head in my wet hand. That's one good thing about velvet goats—they don't care if you get snot on their ears.

"They want me to leave, Tansy. Can you believe that? And me, a Guardian? What are they thinking?"

I had seen a Guardian only once in my life, when we took the boat to Big Crab Island. She was there to heal their hundred-year-old fig tree that had been struck by lightning. In human form, she was so elegant and powerful that I'd thought she must be royalty. Before our eyes, she had transformed into a slinky gleamur. She had scrambled up into the branches and placed her hands on the blackened trunk. A bright light had streamed out of the crack, and the tree was healed.

"I can't do anything like that, Tansy. Look at me! I'm dirty. I'm barefoot. I'm—"

"Talking to a goat."

I turned around to see Grandma. I sniffled. "Talking to Tansy doesn't mean I have powers."

"Maybe." Grandma sighed. "But your grandpa is right, Plum. You *are* special. You don't know it because you've hardly ever left this island and you've got two crusty old people for friends. But there is something about you. I've known it for a long time."

"I don't care if I'm special. I don't want to go."

"I don't want it either," said Grandma quietly. "Plum, I think it's time I give you something." She reached into her apron pocket and brought out a small object. She placed it on my palm.

"A snail shell?" The coils of the honey-colored shell formed a slender, pointed cone. A string of fishing twine ran through a tiny hole in the top.

"Your mother made this when you were still in her belly."

My heart leapt like a grasshopper to hear Grandma talk

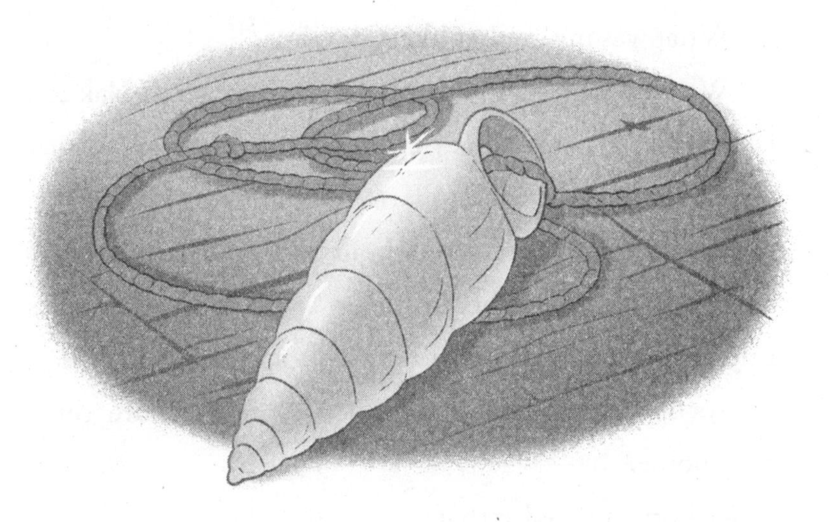

about my mother. I'd never known my parents. I was just a baby when a storm capsized their boat on the open sea.

"She made it after she had a dream about you. She said that she held tight to that dream and put it right inside this shell for you to have when you grew up." Grandma smiled. "I know you're not quite grown. But it's time for you to have it."

I gently traced the coils with my finger. I had always felt like I knew my dad, because Grandma's house was filled with his pictures and old toys. I even slept in his old bed. But we had only one photograph of my mother. I never asked questions about my parents because I didn't want to make Grandma sad. But now it felt like Grandma had opened a door. I had to hurry before it shut again.

"What was my mother like, Grandma?"

"When your dad first brought her here from Nakhon Island, I wasn't sure what to think of her. She was so quiet and small. But she took to farm life right away! She loved to work in the gardens beside your dad. And she loved the sea. They swam together every day after work. Sometimes I thought they would turn into seals and swim away, so I always made something good for dinner to lure them back home."

We both laughed at that.

"I've always thought it was cool that she was from Nakhon Island," I said. "It's such a big, fancy place."

"I'm afraid I don't know much about her life there. She didn't talk about her family, which made me think her past was a sad story. I didn't want to pry. I thought I would have so much more time to get to know her. Now I wish I hadn't waited."

Grandma took both my hands and held them tight like a clamshell. "She loved you so much. So did your dad. They'd both be so proud of how you are growing up."

Grandma was never this talkative. I hung on every word.

"Plum, we have done the best we can for you," she said. "We raised you how your parents would have wanted. But now I think it's time for you to see more of the world. I think they would have wanted that too."

I looked out at the moonlit waves. Our island was perfect in every way. But I also felt something tugging at me, like the tide. As much as I hated to admit it, there was something in me that was curious to go.

"But Grandma . . . being a Guardian? Only a few people ever learn how to do that. What if I can't?"

She squeezed my hand. "Then you'll come back here. This will always be your home. But if you don't try, you'll never know what might have been. Plum, you have—gah! Tansy, get off me!"

Tansy ripped off a chunk of Grandma's apron and swallowed it down.

"Can you take this dang goat with you when you go?"

We both laughed again.

"Here." Grandma took the snail shell out of my hand. "It may look fragile, but it's actually very tough and strong. Just like your mother. Just like you." She tied the twine around my neck, then cupped my face in her steady hands. I tried not to cry because I knew Grandma never did. "This is the right thing to do, Plum. I can feel it in my bones."

I shut my eyes. I wanted to feel it too, but I still wasn't sure. I listened to the night bugs and the frogs singing all around us. I imagined them saying, *Give it a try, give it a try, give it a try.*

"Okay," I said. "I'll give it a try."

CHAPTER 4

"You have your boat ticket?" asked Grandpa as we walked down the hill to our little wooden dock.

"Yes, Grandpa."

"And your jacket?"

"Yes, Grandpa."

"And your hat? Socks? Oh, what about extra underwear?"

"Grandpa!"

My grandma cut him off. "Stop fussing so much. The girl is bringing enough stuff to open her own market! Now, Plum, don't forget this."

She handed me a basket covered with her handkerchief. "I made extra honey egg cakes." She squeezed my hand.

"You can share them with the other kids during the boat ride. Make some new friends."

The large passenger boat swung up beside our dock, and its motor idled, chugging loudly. I had never been on a boat so big before. I grasped the shell pendant around my neck.

"Grandma? What do you think my mother dreamed for me?"

"I don't know," said Grandma softly. "But maybe while you're on Lotus Island, you'll discover the answer."

I threw my arms around her and hugged her tight. Her hair smelled like sweet dough and ginger. "Thank you, Grandma." Then I hugged Grandpa, and he squeezed me so hard it made me laugh. "I love you, Grandpa!"

"Go on, hurry, now," said Grandma. "You don't want to make them wait. And always remember that we—gah! Tansy! How'd you get out of your pen?" She shooed Tansy away from her apron. "Please take this goat with you!"

I nuzzled Tansy one last time. "Take care of them, girl."

I ran down the dock, suitcase in one hand, basket in the other. Before I knew it, I had handed over my ticket and my luggage, and we were shoving off. I stood at the rail and watched as my island became smaller and smaller behind us.

"Goodbye! Goodbye! I love you!"

Grandpa waved with one arm. The other was wrapped around Grandma, who was weeping into his shoulder.

Suddenly I felt a pull on my heart, like a fishing line stretched to breaking. There was so much more I wanted to say to them! But the boat revved its motor, the wind blew my hair back, and my island was only a dot on the horizon, then gone.

CHAPTER 5

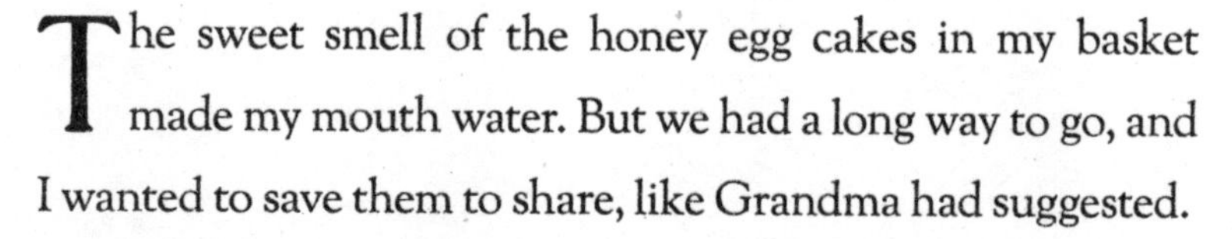

The sweet smell of the honey egg cakes in my basket made my mouth water. But we had a long way to go, and I wanted to save them to share, like Grandma had suggested.

My island, Little Island, was the farthest south in the Santipap Archipelago, and our boat would make stops along the way north to Lotus Island. For the moment I was the only one on board, so I had my pick of seats. I chose one near the rail on the top deck so I could look down and watch the bottle whales racing along in our wake.

"You're all so fast!" I called down to them. "But can you beat us? Go, go!"

I squealed when one of the bottle whales leapt up and flipped its tail, spraying me with water.

The boat attendant came by to punch my ticket. "We should be coming up on Big Crab Island soon. We have one person joining us from there. Then it's on to Nakhon, where we're picking up most of our passengers."

"Thank you, sir." I felt nervous thinking about meeting the other kids. Would they like me? I hugged the basket of egg cakes closer.

When we glided up to the pier at Big Crab Island, a girl with short pigtails and a big backpack got on board. There were fifty empty seats, but she chose one in the row right in front of me.

"The name's Cherry," she said, sticking out her hand. Her eyes were dark and shiny, just like cherries.

I smiled, glad that she had come up to me first. "Nice to meet you. I'm Plum. I guess we can make a fruit salad together?"

Ugh, that was such a cheesy joke! Get it together, Plum!

But Cherry grinned and slapped me on the shoulder. "Ha! I like that! Aren't you just *so* excited to get to the Academy? I can't wait! I've known I would be a Guardian since I was little. But thinking about the lessons and that big test is still a little nerve-wracking, know what I mean?"

I gulped. I didn't know what she meant at all. Big test? Grandpa hadn't said anything about that.

"My uncle is a Guardian," she said with a proud smile. "His Guardian form is a giant narwhale. I guess that means I could end up being a narwhale too." She leaned in and whispered, "But you wanna know a secret?"

I nodded.

"I would love for my Guardian form to be something with big claws, like a jaicat!" She swiped imaginary claws through the air at me and laughed. "What about you? What do you think your Guardian form will be? Hmm, you're kind of quiet, so maybe you'll be some kind of fish or a giant land snail? I guess it all depends on what types of Guardians we turn out to be, so there's no point in getting ahead of ourselves."

I was struggling to keep up with the conversation. I guessed that Cherry had learned all this from her uncle.

"Excuse me, what do you mean by *types* of Guardian?"

"There are three kinds of Guardians: Hand, Heart, and Breath. Hand Guardians are fierce, fast, and strong." She turned to the side and threw some quick air punches. "Heart Guardians are the healers. And Breath Guardians are super chill, and they can calm people down. Or something like that. No one in my family has ever been close to being one of those, haha!" She slapped me on the shoulder again. "But don't worry. No matter what types of Guardian we are, we all learn how to fight."

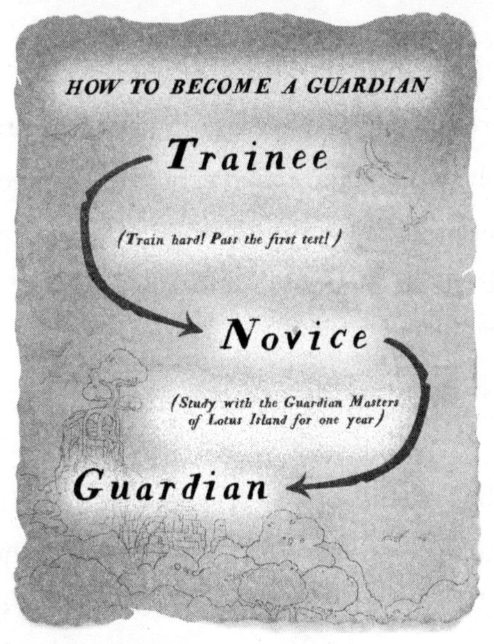

HOW TO BECOME A GUARDIAN
Trainee
(Train hard! Pass the first test!)
Novice
(Study with the Guardian Masters of Lotus Island for one year)
Guardian

"Fight?" I gulped again.

"Sure. As protectors, Guardians have to know about defense. I think it's just a precaution though. We probably won't ever end up actually fighting anyone." Cherry sighed like that was a real tragedy.

She talked on and on, and I learned a lot just from listening to her. For our first month at the Academy, we would be called Trainees. If we did well and passed our first test, we would be promoted to Novices. After one year of training, Novices graduated and became true Guardians.

But that first test was vital. If Trainees didn't pass, they had to go back home.

I suddenly remembered my basket. I held it out to Cherry. "Do you want a honey egg cake? My Grandma made them."

Cherry reached in and pulled out one of the sticky cakes. I thought she would take a nibble, but she popped the entire thing in her mouth!

"Iff faffe fimmy mummy!"

"What?"

She swallowed and wiped her mouth. "It tastes really yummy!"

We both giggled.

"I would give you more, but I need to save them for the other kids," I said, wrapping the rest of the cakes back up.

The boat's motor quieted as it slowed down.

A voice called out over the speaker: "Fifteen minutes to Nakhon Harbor!"

Cherry and I both rushed to the front of the boat and looked out. We were gliding into a huge bay full of boats. An enormous city ringed the harbor with buildings higher than ten of our mango trees stacked on top of one another. I had to shield my eyes from the glare. There was so much glass and so much metal and so many people. I was suddenly very glad we weren't getting off the boat here.

"My mom says everyone who lives in Nakhon is fancy," said Cherry.

"Prepare to take on passengers!" shouted the attendant.

I swallowed. "I guess we're about to find out if that's true."

CHAPTER 6

Our boat attendant said that Nakhon Harbor was too crowded for us to get close to shore, so the next batch of kids would be coming out to us on smaller boats.

"Is that them, coming this way?" I asked Cherry.

A pod of brightly colored objects was skimming toward us across the surface of the water. They were too small to be boats.

"Hoverbots!" Cherry clapped her hands. "Yes! I've always wanted to see the hoverbots of Nakhon!"

The hoverbots were about as tall as me with smooth, rounded bodies. Each one was a different color: dark pink, orange, lime green, bright red, and pineapple yellow. The

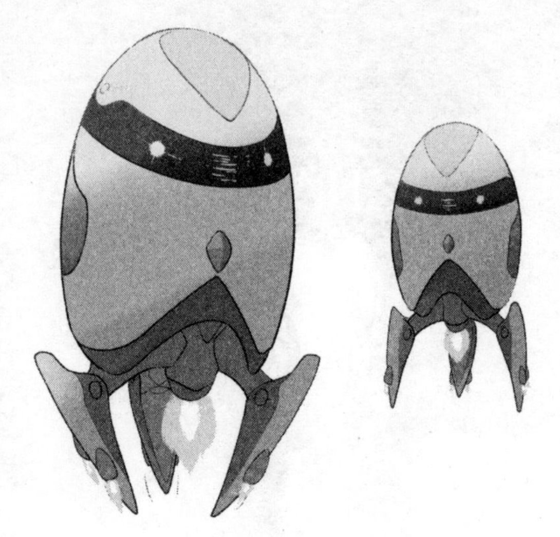

green hoverbot zipped up to the ship, rose above the water, and spoke to our captain.

"Arrival papers requested," it said in a voice that sounded like someone speaking into a glass.

While the captain handed over our arrival papers, the other hoverbots zipped around our boat, repeating "Inspection. Inspection. Inspection."

Suddenly the pink hoverbot flew right up to where Cherry and I stood at the rail. Green beams of light shone out. "Inspection," it said as it scanned the light beams over us. Then it zipped away.

"I guess we passed the inspection?" I whispered to Cherry.

"Cleared to take on passengers," announced the green hoverbot.

And with that, a small white motorboat began whizzing across the harbor toward us. When it got to us, eight new trainees climbed up the ladder and onto the deck of our boat.

They must have been about my age, but they seemed so much older and taller.

As our boat's motor revved up for departure, I hung back, feeling like someone had glued my lips shut. Cherry, on the other hand, walked right up to the other kids and started talking. I wished I could be more like her.

I took a deep breath and picked up my basket. Two girls sat talking in seats under the boat's canopy. They wore brightly colored dresses with sharp pleats. I smoothed down my wrinkled pants as I walked toward them. One of the girls wore her hair in one long braid down her back. I held my hand out to her.

"Hello, my name is Plum. It's so nice to meet you."

The girl with the braid looked at my fingers. "If you expect people to shake your hand, you really should wash it first."

I quickly pulled my hand behind my back. My cheeks burned. I thought I had cleaned my fingernails, but maybe they were still dirty from the garden.

The girl beside her said, "Rella! Mind your manners!" She smiled at me. "My name's Hetty."

Hetty's smile gave me courage. I held the basket out toward them and pulled back the cloth. "It's nice to meet you. Would you like a honey egg cake? My grandmother made them for me to share with everyone."

The girls each took one and said thank you, but I noticed that Rella held hers between her fingers like it was a squashed stink bug. I wanted to run and hide. What was I supposed to say?

Just then we heard a horn blast behind us, and the funny voice of a hoverbot called out, "Cease all motion. Prepare for boarding."

Our boat stopped, and all the kids ran to the rail to see what was going on. A sleek silver speedboat glided up to us, and a tall boy with glasses climbed aboard. He must have been a Trainee too. All the other kids had come aboard alone, like me, but this boy was followed by three grown-ups.

I looked into my basket. I had only one honey egg cake left. My mouth watered, but I felt like I should give mine to him.

As I squared my shoulders and took a step toward him, Rella grabbed my arm. "Please tell me you're not thinking of giving a sticky cake to that boy?" Hetty giggled.

"Don't you know who that is?" asked Rella. "That's

Sam Ubon, the son of Lady Ubon. Their family owns half of Nakhon Island. You really think he's going to want one of your grammy's cakes?"

Hetty leaned toward Rella and whispered, "Did you see the servants come on board with him? Talk about spoiled!"

Rella nodded. "I bet he doesn't even have to blow his own nose."

They laughed and pulled away from me to go back to their seats. Sam Ubon sat toward the front of the boat. None of the other kids, not even Cherry, went up to talk to him. I didn't blame her or anyone else. The servants were fluttering around him like flies while he sat very still. He must have been used to that.

Our boat was off again. As I went to take my seat, I looked into the trash basket near the rail.

The honey egg cakes I had given to the girls lay smashed at the bottom. Neither of them had even taken a bite.

CHAPTER 7

Our boat continued through the Santipap Islands, stopping here and there to pick up more Trainees. None of the kids we picked up were as well dressed as the ones from Nakhon, and definitely no one had servants in tow like Sam. But no one else was like me either. They all seemed to have worn their best clothes and new shoes. I was wearing my gardening clogs, which were a half size too small so that my heels stuck out the back.

But Cherry didn't seem to notice any of that. She included me in every conversation. I started to think I could call her my friend, though truly she was friends with everyone. She chattered and threw her head back and laughed and laughed. It was so easy to be around her.

I tried to listen in on everyone's conversations about the Guardian Academy. It seemed like they all knew someone who had gone there in the past—a cousin, a grandparent, or someone from their village. But even so, no one seemed to know exactly what our training would be like or what the first test would be, just that you did not want to fail it.

I was listening to Cherry tell an exciting story about her uncle's adventures as a narwhale when suddenly one of the kids pointed and shouted, "Look, is that it?"

We all rushed to the front railing, even Sam, whose servant ran after him, holding an umbrella over his head to block the sun.

"Wow," said Cherry. "Lotus Island! It's just like I imagined it!"

I hadn't known what to imagine, but the moment I saw Lotus Island, I felt like I had seen it in my dreams all my life. Birds dived down the faces of sheer gray cliffs that towered above the water. It was green, so green, with trees growing between the massive rocks. The late afternoon sun glinted off the gold tiles of the rooftops, making the whole island glow.

I glanced at Rella, who stood beside me. She was mesmerized too. It almost seemed like she might start crying. I

knew how she felt. I touched my shell necklace, wondering what my mother would think if she could see me now.

The boat pulled up to a dock that jutted out from a long sandy beach. We all lined up to gather our bags.

Two people stood on the dock to meet us: a young man wearing golden-brown robes, and a woman with short hair and a white tunic and pants. We bowed to them as we stepped onto the dock.

"Welcome, new Trainees, welcome to Lotus Island!" said

the young man. "My name is Brother Chalad, and I'm one of the instructors here. This is Master Dew, another one of our teachers."

The woman in white greeted us with a wink. "Welcome, little sisters and brothers. We're happy you're here. We will have a ceremony tonight to properly welcome you to the island. But first we'll show you to your rooms and let you rest."

It had been a very long day for me, but my whole body buzzed with excitement as I followed behind the other kids.

Brother Chalad hung back to speak with Sam's servants. "I'm sorry, but only new Trainees are allowed onto the island at this time," Brother Chalad said. "I'm afraid you'll have to return to the boat."

The servant with the umbrella frowned. "But Lady Ubon herself sent me! Surely Master Sunback will make an exception for us!"

Brother Chalad smiled and shook his head. "I'm afraid that's impossible. If young Sam wants to begin his training, he has to do it alone. I would think Lady Ubon knows the rules."

"Plum, are you coming?" Cherry called.

I jogged to catch up to her.

When we reached the end of the dock, I looked back to see the servants returning to the boat and Brother Chalad helping Sam with his many bags.

Rella snickered. "Let's see how the little prince does without his court."

CHAPTER 8

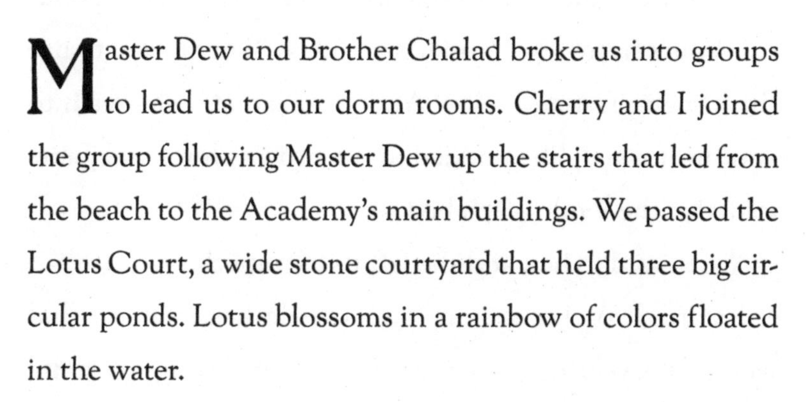

Master Dew and Brother Chalad broke us into groups to lead us to our dorm rooms. Cherry and I joined the group following Master Dew up the stairs that led from the beach to the Academy's main buildings. We passed the Lotus Court, a wide stone courtyard that held three big circular ponds. Lotus blossoms in a rainbow of colors floated in the water.

I had imagined the Guardian Academy would be one large building, like the school on Big Crab Island. Instead we walked past many small structures that sat along the edges of the cliffs. Some were even carved right into the cliffs themselves! Master Dew led us down paths and through gardens filled with flowers I had never seen before.

Finally we stopped in front of a large wooden building surrounded by mango trees.

"This is one of our dorms," said Master Dew. She began assigning Trainees to their rooms. By the end, Cherry, Rella, Hetty, and I were the only ones left. "You four—follow me upstairs."

Our room was on the second floor. It was simple, with polished wood floors and thick sleeping mats arranged against the walls. A large round window looked out over the gardens behind our building.

"Our welcome ceremony starts at sunset, which is about two hours from now," said Master Dew. "I invite you to use this time to rest and relax. And go ahead and change into your uniforms." She nodded to the brown shirts and pants folded at the foot of each bed.

We bowed to her, and she left us to unpack.

I started to change into my new clothes, grateful that we'd all be wearing the same thing. Maybe I wouldn't stand out so much.

Hetty held her uniform up and wrinkled her nose. "Do they have to be so . . . plain?"

"So, what should we do for the next couple of hours?" asked Cherry. She dove onto her mat and bounced on her knees. "Who's up for wrestling? If anyone can pin me longer than three seconds, I'll give you my dessert for a week."

Rella had already changed. She stood beside the window, looking down. "Do they really expect us to spend all this time resting? We're not babies. I want to have a look around."

"Too bad we can't jump down and explore," said Hetty.

"Well, why can't we?" said Rella. She leaned out the window. Thick vines covered the outside of our building. Rella gave one of the vines a tug.

Hetty gasped. "You mean break the rules? Already?"

Rella shrugged. "They didn't say it was a *rule* that we couldn't leave. They just *invited us* to rest. That doesn't mean we have to." She swung her legs over the window ledge.

"Wait!" I said, rushing over to her.

Rella rolled her eyes at me. "Don't give me a lecture."

"You're going to fall!" I nodded to the vine she gripped. "That's a clingsuckle vine, and as soon as you put weight on it, the suckers will unstick from the wall and you'll go tumbling."

Rella narrowed her eyes at me. "Yeah, right, farmer girl."

Why did she dislike me so much? Part of me wanted to cry, and part of me—a big part—wanted to show Rella up.

I climbed onto the window ledge and took hold of a thicker vine. "If you're going to do it, at least use the cobra grape. Or maybe you don't know what that is since you don't live on a farm." I climbed down the vine quickly, knowing that a cobra grapevine was strong enough to hold an elephant.

I dropped to the ground and wiped my hands on my pants. Soon the other three girls had climbed down after me, even Hetty.

Rella smiled at me. "Wow, Plum, I didn't take you for a rule breaker. That's pretty cool of you."

I frowned. Rule breaker? Maybe Hetty was right and we should go back. But before I could say anything, Cherry tapped me on the shoulder. "Let's just look around for a little bit, okay?"

"Okay."

I guess I was a rule breaker after all.

CHAPTER 9

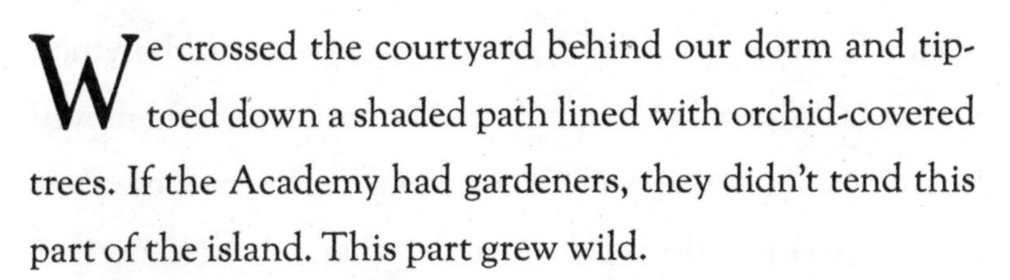

We crossed the courtyard behind our dorm and tiptoed down a shaded path lined with orchid-covered trees. If the Academy had gardeners, they didn't tend this part of the island. This part grew wild.

Soon the path ended at the edge of a dense grove of trees. I peered into the dark green shadows.

"Looks like this is where the Academy ends and the jungle begins," I said.

"Maybe we should go back," said Hetty.

"Hold on," said Rella. "Why would the path lead us here and then just stop? There has to be a way through."

While the others searched the edge of the forest, I walked up to an enormous yamyam tree. Plump yamyam fruits grew straight out of the reddish-brown bark. Its trunk was so big around, it must have been more than a hundred years old. Thick vines hung down from its branches like curtains. My grandparents had always taught me that trees this ancient were elders and should be respected.

I placed my hands together and bowed to the tree. "Hello, Grandmother Yamyam," I whispered. "I hope we aren't disturbing you. We would love to explore your forest, but of course we wouldn't dare to do so without your permission." I shut my eyes and bowed lower.

I heard a rustling sound. I opened my eyes and straightened. To my surprise, there was a path between the vines. It was as if the old tree had shifted her branches and moved the vines out of the way. When I looked down, there were stones peeking through the moss that I hadn't noticed before.

"Cherry! Rella! Hetty!" I called. "I found a path!"

Rella bounded over. "Nice work, Plum. You go first." She put her hand on my back and pushed me forward. I swallowed and started walking.

"I hope this is all right," I whispered to the forest. "We won't hurt anything. We're just passing through."

"Who are you talking to?" asked Rella.

"Um, nobody."

A soft breeze blew through the trees, and the branches and vines seemed to make way for us. Soon we reached a sunny clearing where the trees thinned out. I heard the trickling of water nearby.

"Look at that!" said Rella. She pushed in front of me and ran ahead. A large building made of moss-covered stones loomed over us. It had been built right into the mountainside. Half of it lay in ruins.

"Be careful!" said Hetty.

"Whoa . . ." said Cherry. "This place looks *old*."

"Come see *this*!" called Rella.

She stood in one of the large doorways that led into the building. Carefully we walked inside. We stood in a long open room. The far wall was covered in a painted mural that stretched from the floor to the ceiling. The paint was fading, but we could see colorful images of people, boats, islands, and all sorts of animals.

"This looks like an old temple," said Rella.

Hetty ran her finger tenderly over the paintings. "This mural tells the legends of Lotus Island and the Guardians," she whispered, "and how they came here from the Old Home."

A shiver went down my spine. I loved the few stories I had heard about the Old Home. "Do you know the legends?" I asked.

Hetty nodded. "My father's a librarian on Nakhon Island, and he's studied the old stories."

"Well?" said Cherry. "Tell us!"

"Long ago," Hetty began, "when the Earth was young and magic was everywhere, our people lived in a place called the Old Home. It was perfect. A paradise. But over time, humans became selfish and greedy, and they fought wars that began to destroy the Old Home. The animals of the world held a big meeting. Humans were becoming too powerful, and some of the animals argued that they should destroy the humans before humans destroyed the world. Other animals defended their human cousins and pressed for peace."

Hetty continued, "The Great Beast offered a compromise: He would take the animals away from the Old Home to a safe place where they could live in harmony. The only humans allowed to come with them had to swear an oath to protect all living things. They all climbed aboard the Great Beast's back, and he took them far, far away to the Santipap Sea."

In the mural, the Great Beast had the body of a sea dragon, the head of a lion, wings of a bird, and the tail of a fish.

"Is this for real?" asked Cherry, her eyes wide.

"Hush and listen," said Hetty. "The journey took all the Great Beast's strength, and he was nearly spent by the time they arrived. He gave the last of his power to the humans, granting them the ability to transform into magical creatures who could defend the animals if they were ever in danger. These humans became the first Guardians, and they took their power from the Great Beast's hands, heart, and breath. After that, the Great Beast lay down in the sea, and the humps of his back became the Santipap Islands."

Hand. Heart. Breath. Just like the three types of Guardians.

Cherry clapped. I smiled and clapped too. Hetty was a wonderful storyteller.

"But wait," I said. "Does that mean that all of us who live in Santipap are related to those first Guardians?"

Hetty nodded. "That's right. But over the centuries, humans let their powers fade, and most lost them altogether. That's why this Academy exists: to find those of us who still have a spark of power and teach us how to use it."

I expected Rella to roll her eyes at this story, but she was kneeling at the bottom of the mural, peering at the designs that had been scrawled onto the wall with glimmering gold paint. "Imagine all that magic from the Great Beast, just lost," she said. "If I had power like that, I'd never let it go."

I looked at the paintings for a little while longer, then went back outside to breathe in the fresh scents of the forest. I followed the sound of trickling water to a sunny spot where I found a small pond filled with lotus plants. The buds were closed tight, like pale green paintbrushes. I could tell that the pond was natural, not built by human hands.

I breathed deeply. It was so peaceful. I felt like I could sit there for hours and be happy.

Behind me, I heard a rustle. "Cherry!" I said. "Come see, this pond is so pretty!"

I turned around. "Cherry?" I saw a flash of gold-orange scales. A long, thick tail slithered behind a bush and disappeared into the shadows. My throat went dry. "Rella? Hetty?"

I stood up and ran to go find them and bumped straight into an old woman. I bowed quickly. "Oh, I'm so sorry, ma'am. I hope I didn't hurt you."

The woman lifted her wrinkled face. She had short-cropped hair as white as a dandelion puff. She wore a mud-splashed tunic and held a basket full of lotus buds in one hand and clipping shears in the other.

Just then, Hetty, Cherry, and Rella came running over. When they saw I was talking to someone, their eyes grew wide.

The old woman tilted her head at us. "If I'm not mistaken, all the Trainees have been asked to rest before the welcome ceremony. There are places you shouldn't go on Lotus Island."

Hetty pointed at me, lips trembling. "Plum climbed out the window! We told her not to, but she wouldn't listen!"

Rella folded her arms. Her eyes roved over the woman's dirty clothes. "We didn't break any rules. And I don't believe it's the place of the gardening staff to tell us what to do. We'll take this matter up with Master Sunback."

The woman clipped one more lotus bud and stuck it in her basket. "No need. She already knows." She smiled broadly at us. "So nice to meet you, my dears. I am Master Sunback."

I gulped.

"Come," she said. "Since you are so well rested already, we might as well put you to work."

Cherry and I exchanged a worried look. We hadn't been here more than three hours, and we'd already gotten on the bad side of the Academy's headmaster.

Hetty yawned as she passed me another plate to polish. "I'm so tired! I wish we had rested!"

We were in the kitchens, where Master Sunback had led us to get the dishes ready for the evening meal. I yawned too. I felt like I could fall asleep on my feet.

Cherry seemed as energetic as ever. "It was totally worth it to see those cool ruins! And that awesome mural."

Rella leaned against the counter and watched us work. "I want to go back."

Hetty's eyes grew wide. "But Master Sunback said there were places we shouldn't go. It could be dangerous!"

Brother Chalad poked his head into the kitchen. "I think

you've done enough, girls. Come on, the ceremony is about to start."

We followed him out to the Lotus Court, where the other Trainees had already gathered. I counted fifteen of us wearing brown uniforms, including Sam Ubon, who stood apart from everyone else.

Cherry leaned over and whispered to me, "Did you hear that Sam has his own dorm?"

"Wow, he gets his own room?"

"No, he gets his own *dorm.* The whole building all to himself! Must be nice to have a rich mom."

These kids from Nakhon Island. Before today I had never even thought about money, but here it seemed to be part of nearly every conversation I had.

The sun had set now, and the ocean was dark. Tiny lights began to twinkle above the lotus ponds.

"Twile-flies!" I said to Cherry. "I used to chase them back home with Tansy!"

Master Dew stepped out into the court, and we all bowed to her in greeting. "Good evening, young friends. We now welcome you officially as Trainees at the Guardian Academy on Lotus Island!" She waited for our applause to die down. "It is now my great pleasure to introduce our Academy's headmaster, Master Sunback."

Of course, the four of us had met Master Sunback already, but this time she was dressed in a long white robe with an orange belt tied in a fancy knot.

I wondered how old she was. Her hair was whiter than my grandma's, and her skin was wrinklier. But there was something young about the way she moved and the playful look in her eyes when she smiled.

"Welcome, children, welcome," she said, holding her hands out to us. "This is a very special night, one that we have been looking forward to for ten long years. You have been selected as Trainees because you show potential to possess the power of the Guardians. For the next month, you will receive instruction in the arts of caretaking, meditation, and defense. This training will help you connect with your Guardian forms."

Master Sunback pointed to the full moon. "By the next full moon, you will be tested to see if you can change into your Guardian form. This is the first and most important test on the path to becoming a Guardian. If you pass, you will become a Novice, and you will stay here to continue your training."

She smiled, and deep wrinkles creased the corners of her eyes. "Now, don't let me keep blabbering on. It is time to meet a very special group of people. They have traveled from the far reaches of our islands to show you what awaits you."

Master Sunback stepped aside, and a line of six young men and women marched out of one of the side pavilions. They all walked tall and square-shouldered.

"Oh, they must be the Guardians who were Novices before us!" whispered Cherry.

The Guardians formed a line in front of Master Sunback and greeted us with smiles. The air seemed to crackle with magic.

"It is important that Guardians learn to master every element of our craft," said Master Sunback. "But there will be one element that comes most naturally to you. You may demonstrate great strength and agility and become a Hand Guardian . . ."

Two Guardians stepped forward and raised their arms high. They swooped their arms down, and in an instant they transformed.

One became a zorahawk with broad wings and a curved beak. The other was a glister mare with a sparkling mane and powerful legs. The mare galloped across the lotus court so fast that she became a streak of silver. The zorahawk gripped a heavy boulder in his talons and carried it easily from one end of the courtyard to the other.

We all gasped and cheered.

Master Sunback smiled. "Or perhaps you will become a Heart Guardian, with the skills to nurture and heal . . ."

The next two Guardians stepped forward and transformed into a buttermoth and a golden raccoon. Together they knelt at the edge of one of the lotus ponds, where the sun had scorched the lotus pads a patchy brown. The raccoon placed his hands on the damaged leaves while the buttermoth fluttered her wings. Green life flowed back into the pads, healing them completely.

We clapped in awe.

"Or perhaps you will be a Breath Guardian," said Master Sunback, "with powers of the mind and the senses."

The last two Guardians transformed into the same thing: wingrays. They glided through the air as easily as if they were swimming through the sea. They beat their great leathery wings, creating a cool breeze. When the air hit us, a sense of calm washed over me. Both Cherry and I breathed deep sighs of happiness.

"Calming people down is a cool power to have," Cherry whispered to me.

"Totally cool."

The twile-flies swirled out of the lotus blossoms and hovered over our heads. I could hardly believe these amazing Guardians in front of us had been in our place ten years ago. Could I really learn how to become something as wonderful as them?

Master Sunback raised her hands and clapped twice. All the Guardians resumed their human forms. We gave them a huge round of applause.

"Now, my Trainees, you have seen what lies ahead," said Master Sunback. "You must choose whether to undertake this journey. If you do not accept, no one will blame you. But if you choose to stay for the first test, please take a lotus bud and place it in the water."

She held up the basket of pale green buds I had seen her collecting from the pond by the ruins. One by one, she called our names. When Cherry was called, she confidently strode up to Master Sunback and took her flower.

My turn was coming. Behind me, Rella whispered to someone, "This Guardian stuff is tough. Not for just any old farm girl."

My ears burned. Oh, how I wanted to prove her wrong!

But being a Guardian was a huge responsibility. I couldn't take it on just to spite Rella. I looked up at the row of adult Guardians. They seemed so confident and sure, like they knew exactly what their place was in the world. I wanted that for myself. I clutched my shell pendant and shut my eyes.

"Plum?" said Master Sunback. "Plum, have you decided?"

I walked forward, took my flower, and floated it in the water beside the others.

All around me, the twile-flies blinked to the beat of my racing heart.

The next morning, all the Trainees were so excited to begin.

"Welcome to your very first Heart class," said Brother Chalad with a smile. "Your Heart training will teach you the art of healing and caring for the living things of this world. Heart Guardians have the power to mend broken bones, soothe pain, and repair damage."

Cherry raised her hand. "Brother Chalad, my neighbor says that Heart Guardians can bring people back from the brink of death."

Everyone whispered curiously about this, but Brother Chalad shook his head. "That is an old legend, but I have never known a Guardian who was able to do something so powerful. And today we will certainly be starting with something much less complicated. Follow me!"

He led us past the dorm buildings, along the edge of the forest, and into a large sunny meadow. A stream trickled out of the forest and burbled among the grasses.

Brother Chalad pushed the sleeves of his robe up and held out his palms. With a twitch of his nose, he transformed into a fluffy lemon kinkajou with a yellow-and-white-striped tail. We all burst into applause. I was glad I wasn't the only one who still got breathless to see Guardians transform.

Brother Chalad held up his little kinkajou hands to quiet us down. "One of the most important parts of the healing arts is making medicines from plants and herbs. Some of these are very rare and difficult to find, such as frailbane."

He dropped down on all fours and snuffled around in the tall grass. After a moment he stood up on his back legs with a tiny purple flower clamped in his teeth. He stretched up and changed back into his human form, holding the flower out for all of us to see.

"Today you won't need to find anything nearly as rare as this," said Brother Chalad as he gently tucked the flower into his satchel. "You will start with common herbs. Work with a partner. The first team who gathers everything on their list gets an extra five points on their assignment."

The Trainees began partnering up as Brother Chalad handed out lists. I wanted to be with Cherry, but another girl had already asked her. One boy from Nakhon Island didn't have a partner yet. Would he want to work with a farm girl like me?

I puffed up my lungs and tapped him on the shoulder. "I'm Plum. Do you want to work together?"

"Yeah, sure. My name's Salan." He shook my hand very formally. "The first plant on the list is peelie milkfoot." He pointed to the paper. Beside each plant's name there was a little sketch of what it looked like. "Should we start searching up there, on that hill?"

"Well, milkfoot likes to grow in wet soil," I said, "so we probably want to try near the stream for that one."

Salan tilted his head at me. "How do you know that?"

Grandma had taught me about all these herbs before I could even read. But I said, "Um, I have a book about plants at home."

We headed to the stream, and sure enough, clumps of peelie milkfoot grew along the water's edge. We also gathered riverwort and seethen nearby.

I pointed at the next plant on the list. "Oh, fafarrel, I know what that looks like! Let's look on the hill—it clings to sunny rocks."

This was almost too easy. Salan was a great partner and a fast learner. We laughed as we raced up the hill together.

"Plum, I think I found it," called Salan as he turned over a smooth stone. "Is this—ow!"

"What happened?"

He rubbed the back of his hand. "An ant bit me! Oh, this really stings!"

I searched around in the shade of the biggest stones. *Dark green leaves with veins of blue, it's gotta be here . . . where is it . . . there!*

I plucked the dark leaves, shoved them in my mouth, and started to chew.

"Uh, what are you doing?" asked Salan.

"This is itchbane," I said as I chewed the leaves into a pulp. "It'll stop the stinging right away. Here."

I took the green mash out of my mouth and stuck it onto Salan's ant bite.

"EWWW!" cried Salan. "What the—"

Oh gosh, what had I done? Now Salan would really think I was weird!

“Hey,” Salan said. He flexed his fingers. “Hey, that is . . . whoa, the stinging is gone. Plum, you’re amazing! Did you learn this from your book too?”

I breathed a sigh of relief and smiled. “Actually . . . my grandma taught me.”

“Well, it’s super cool,” said Salan. “But next time? Let me chew up my own itchbane, okay?”

I laughed, and we ran to tell Brother Chalad that we were the first to finish. If all our training was going to be this easy, then I would pass our first test, no problem.

Next up was Hand class. Master Dew greeted us on the wide grassy lawn between the Lotus Court and the kitchens.

"Hand Guardians never attack unprovoked," she said, "but sometimes our work takes us into dangerous situations, and we must be prepared to defend ourselves and those around us."

A boy named Twist raised his hand. "Excuse me, Master Dew, but shouldn't we be learning defense in our Guardian forms?"

Master Dew nodded and smiled. "If you pass the first test and become a Novice, you will definitely learn how to defend yourself in your Guardian form. But everything I teach you in this class will be useful no matter what form you are in. And if for some reason you lose the ability to transform, you'll be able to defend yourself as a human."

We all cast curious looks at one another. Until then, no one had mentioned that a Guardian could *lose* their powers.

Cherry stood up and bounced to the front of the class. "I'm ready! I'm ready! Let's do this! What's first? Flying kicks? Punches? Combination flying punch-kicks?"

Master Dew's mouth twitched up in a smile. She dropped into a crouch, and when she sprang back up, she transformed into a huge muscular jaicat with an inky coat and a pair of short golden horns perched between her ears.

She prowled in a slow circle around Cherry, and then—before any of us could blink—she pounced on her, tackling Cherry onto her back.

Cherry grunted and squirmed as the jaicat leaned her paws on her shoulders.

"Can you throw a punch now?" Master Dew asked Cherry. "How about a kick?" She laughed as Cherry struggled. "If you can't escape, you don't stand much of a chance against me."

"I can't escape!" said Cherry. "It's impossible!"

With a shake of her head, Master Dew transformed back into a human. She reached her hand out to Cherry and helped her up. "It *is* possible. And it is vital that you learn how." She turned to address the entire class. "Escape means survival. If you pay attention in this class, you will learn how to escape from almost any situation. Knowing you can escape will give you the confidence to face even the toughest opponent." She put her hand on Cherry's shoulder. "Am I right, Cherry?"

Cherry smiled and nodded. "Right."

"Well, then, let's get started!"

That's when we learned that we'd be spending most of Hand class squirming around on the ground.

Master Dew taught us how to bridge our hips to shift an opponent's center of gravity and topple them. We learned which of our muscle groups were the strongest, and we learned how to use them against an opponent to gain an advantage. Leverage and balance were way more important than strength or size. With those two skills, even a small person could escape from someone much bigger and stronger.

By the end of class, we had learned two basic escape moves. I was surprised by how much we had improved in such a short time. But no one was as good as Rella. Every time Hetty tried to pin her down, she slipped out within seconds and was up on her feet.

"Look at how Rella keeps her eyes on Hetty's face," said Cherry. "That way she can tell what move Hetty's about to make before she makes it. She's always one step ahead. Smart."

"Yeah, she is," I said with a frown.

By the time we got to our third and last class of the day—Breath—we were all tired but excited. We chattered like songbirds as we waited for Master Sunback to join us in the covered pavilion on the Lotus Court.

"When do you think they'll teach us how to transform?" asked Salan.

"Ooh, maybe we'll learn today!" said Hetty.

Cherry leaned toward them. "My uncle told me that when you're first learning, only parts of your body transform."

A boy named Mikko looked worried. "What if you grow a tail and you can't change back? And then you have to walk around with a deer butt for the whole day?"

We heard a chuckle behind us. We turned and bowed as Master Sunback stepped into the pavilion. "You'll be pleased to know that I have never had a deer butt incident in my class, Mikko. Now, everyone, please sit comfortably, and we will get started."

I settled in next to Cherry. This time I was the one bouncing in place. I couldn't wait to find out what cool things we'd be doing.

"Close your eyes," said Master Sunback. "Begin by noticing your breathing. Focus on the place just inside your nostrils, and feel your breath go into your nose and out. Breathe in through your nose, and out through your nose."

This is it, I thought. *In just a moment, she'll teach us the secret to harnessing our Guardian powers . . .*

But she didn't. For the entire class, we practiced breathing in and out. And that was . . . it. When I finally opened my eyes, I saw that the other kids around me also wore looks of disappointment.

Master Sunback opened her eyes and exhaled with a smile. "Good work, young Trainees. Most of you need much more practice, but that's enough for today. Time for lunch."

"Was that really it?" I whispered to Cherry.

"Maybe it was just a warm-up class?"

"I don't need to learn to breathe!" huffed Rella as we walked to the dining hall. "I've been breathing all my life. What a waste of time!"

I hated to admit it, but I sort of agreed with Rella.

CHAPTER 13

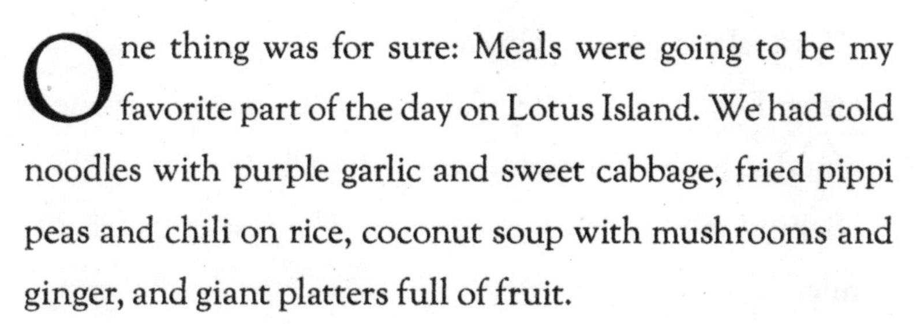

One thing was for sure: Meals were going to be my favorite part of the day on Lotus Island. We had cold noodles with purple garlic and sweet cabbage, fried pippi peas and chili on rice, coconut soup with mushrooms and ginger, and giant platters full of fruit.

"Hey, Plum," said Cherry, stuffing her mouth with longans, "we could sit in the bowl when it's empty, and we'd be a fruit salad! Remember?"

We all laughed. The other great thing about lunch was getting to know the other kids. I had already met clever Salan and goofy Mikko. There was Emmie, a shy girl from Windy Island. Twist showed us that he could put forty-one sassberries in his mouth at once. There were the twins—Basil and

Drum—who looked identical except for Basil's freckles. Most of the Nakhon Island kids ate at their own table. Then there was Sam, who sat at a table by himself.

I stuffed a piece of papaya in my mouth and suddenly felt exhausted. But we had one last thing on our schedule.

"What do you think Community Fun Time is?" I asked.

"I hope it's swimming at the beach, because I'm boiling!" said Twist.

"Maybe it's playing games," said Emmie.

"Or taking a nap," said Mikko with a big yawn.

It turned out that Community Fun Time was chores.

"Our island prospers because we all take care of it," said Master Dew with a cheerful smile. "I know everyone is excited to hear what their chore will be."

Behind me I heard some groans. The rest of us tried to smile.

"Cherry and Rella, head to the kitchen to start washing up from lunch," said Master Dew. "Salan and Hetty, you can help clean the linens. You kids over there can help me sweep up the Lotus Court and pavilions. And Sam and Plum, you two head to the kitchen gardens for weeding."

I frowned. I didn't mind doing chores, but did I have to be paired with Snobby Sam? He bowed to Master Dew and walked toward the gardens without even waiting for me.

❧

Lotus Island's vegetable gardens were planted on a hill that sloped gently up toward a grove of bample trees. The gardens were much bigger than ours back home. Plump tomatoes and shiny eggplants hung in heavy clusters. There were many rows of dark green vegetables and tall trellises covered in beans.

"Afternoon," said a man wearing brown robes. "I'm Brother Dan. I take care of the kitchen garden. Take these gloves, and you can start wherever you think needs the most work."

I passed one pair of gloves to Sam. "How about you start with the beans, and I'll take the cabbages? Do you have a lot of experience in gardens?"

He mumbled something I couldn't hear and headed for the beans.

Fine. If he didn't want to talk to me, then I didn't want to talk to him either.

I knelt down among the bright purple cabbages and got started. Suddenly I felt a sharp pang of missing Grandma and Grandpa. But I was determined not to cry, especially not in front of Sam.

Pretty soon, sweat was dripping off the end of my nose. It felt good to be digging my hands through the dark, fluffy soil. I was lost in it and didn't give a thought to Rella, being a Guardian, or anything else about Lotus Island.

I guess I was pretty into my work, because I fell into my old habit of talking to the creatures around me.

"Hey, worm friends, you like this pepper patch, huh? Well, good, do your best so we can have some spicy chilis in our sauce. Oh, hey, whippertail," I said to the little bird that landed on a nearby cherrycorn stalk. "Now, don't go eating these worms, okay? They're doing us a big favor. But I know you must have some chicks in your nest to feed. There are some juicy spikebeetles that are attacking our tomatoes. Not gonna say more than that, but you know what to do."

The whippertail bobbed her head at me and flew off toward the tomatoes. I followed her flight with a smile.

That's when I noticed Sam kneeling in the melon patch, watching me. He quickly looked away when he realized I had seen him.

Great. Now he was sure to tell the others that I was a ridiculous farm girl who talked to worms, and I'd never hear the end of it from Rella.

Why did worms always give me so much trouble?

CHAPTER 14

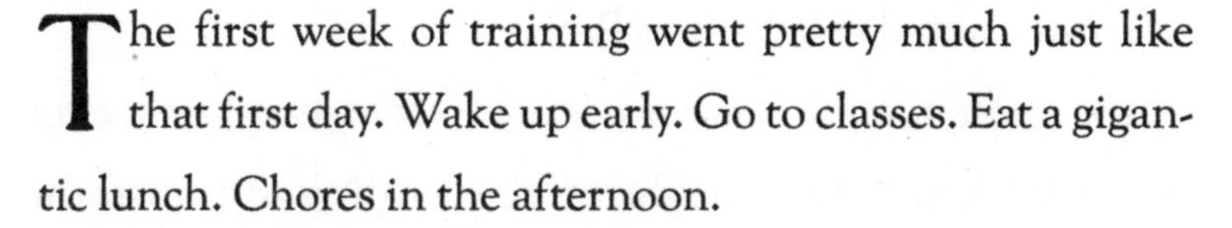

The first week of training went pretty much just like that first day. Wake up early. Go to classes. Eat a gigantic lunch. Chores in the afternoon.

Our classes continued to be . . . well, kind of boring. I didn't complain, but I couldn't blame my fellow Trainees for being impatient.

"Brother Chalad, aren't we supposed to be *healing* the animals?" asked Mikko. "Not just watching them?"

"Healing begins with paying attention," said Brother Chalad. "So take your clipboard and write down everything these slugs are trying to tell you."

In Hand class, we still hadn't thrown a single kick or punch. But we had climbed the three hundred steps that led up to the Sunrise Temple a dozen times. Master Dew said it would build our strength and stamina. So far, I had built blisters on both feet, and my legs felt like jelly. Unlike Cherry, I was glad we weren't fighting, because my muscles were too sore to do anything but sit.

I also missed Grandma and Grandpa so much it made my stomach hurt. But I knew that if I passed the first test, I would make them so proud. I wanted that more than anything.

I also wanted to stick it to Rella.

I was not going to let her have the satisfaction of seeing me fail. I hated the thought of her learning to transform faster than me. But so far, despite all our work, none of the Trainees had transformed yet.

"The only thing I'm going to transform into is a sleeping person," said Salan as we sat on our mats waiting for Master Sunback.

"Let me guess," said Hetty with a sigh. "We'll be breathing again today."

Rella stood up. "I know how to breathe. I think I've been doing a pretty good job of it so far."

"What are you doing?" asked Cherry.

"There has to be a better way to uncover our Guardian powers," said Rella. "I'm not going to waste my time sitting around."

Master Sunback arrived, and Rella bowed low to her.

"Apologies, Master Sunback, but I'm not feeling well," said Rella in a meek-sounding voice. "I think I should go lay down."

"Lie," said Master Sunback.

We all held our breath. Did Master Sunback know that Rella wasn't telling the truth?

But then the old woman smiled and said, "The correct word is that you are going to *lie* down, Rella. Not lay."

Rella smiled nervously, then bowed again and left.

Master Sunback took a seat at the front of the class. "We return to the breath," she said. "Let the rest of the world fall away until there is nothing left but your breathing."

I began breathing in and out slowly with the others, just as we had every day. And just as it did every day, my mind started to whir with thoughts:

Why does Rella hate me so much?

If I do transform into a giant land snail, will she laugh at me?

What if I fail and disappoint Grandma and Grandpa?

What if I never find out my mother's dream for me?

These types of worries had started to spin in my brain all the time, even when I lay down to sleep. I had also started having dreams about the first test. In every dream, I was the only one who didn't know what to do.

That night I woke from that same dream, my hair soaked with sweat. I rolled over and blinked. It was still dark out, so it took me a moment to realize something felt off.

That's when I noticed that Rella wasn't in her bed.

I tried to stay awake to see if Rella came back to bed, but I accidentally fell asleep. The next morning, I watched her at breakfast, but she seemed normal. I wondered how she could appear so relaxed when she was skipping class. Wasn't she nervous about the first test too? But I couldn't worry about her; I needed to worry about myself. The only time I ever felt relaxed was during chores.

Our chore schedule was supposed to rotate, but Sam and I stayed assigned to the garden. I didn't know why—it seemed like the teachers had made a mistake. But I didn't complain. I liked hanging out in the garden.

If I had been paired up with a different person, we probably would have become good friends by now. But Sam hardly ever said a word to me. I was too tired and preoccupied worrying about the first test to care.

In the evenings, we had small meals—usually soup or omelets on rice. Every night Cherry and I made plans to stay up late talking, and every night we passed out as soon as we hit our mats. Sunrise always came way too soon.

"I can't do it," said Cherry, lying like a starfish on her mat. It was early in the morning, two weeks before the first test. "Just leave me here. I'll face the wrath of Master Dew, but I can't get up before the sun one more time."

"Oh, that's too bad," I said. "I heard that today in Hand class, we're finally practicing kicks."

Cherry hopped out of bed and threw on her clothes so fast she put them on backward.

~

But first we had Heart class.

Brother Chalad greeted us by saying, "Today we will be listening to sea cucumbers."

We all groaned, and he laughed at us until tears came out of his eyes. "You should see your faces! Ah, that joke never gets old! Seriously, though, today we start the third week of your training, which means things start to ratchet up."

We all looked at one another, wondering what he meant.

Brother Chalad led us to a grassy pasture behind the kitchen garden.

"Today we will finally begin to work in the healing arts," he said. "And we will be starting with . . ."

He swung open the little wooden gate that led to the pasture.

"Dough lambs!"

A dozen fluffy white puffballs bounced and rolled through the gate and bounded toward us. Their noses and ears were flecked with brown, like someone had sprinkled cinnamon on them.

"Oh my gosh, dough lambs are the cutest!" cried Hetty as one of the sweet lambs licked her face.

"They are cute," said Brother Chalad, "but they are *not* good listeners. And they want to go everywhere and nibble everything. They are in this special pen because they got into a patch of wild parsnicks, which are highly poisonous. We have to feed them an antidote every day, or they could get very sick. Today your assignment is to convince them to take their medicine." He laughed again and slapped his leg. "Oh boy, this is going to be entertaining!"

Brother Chalad handed us each a wooden bowl filled with a stinky green paste. Right away I understood why he had laughed at us. My lamb wanted to eat everything in sight . . . except her medicine. I needed a name for her. I chose Mip because that was the sound she made when she spotted a potential snack.

"No, Mip, not the garden! Come take your medicine!"

I chased her out of the cilantro beds only to find her crashing through the beans. I saw Salan and asked if he was having better luck.

He held up his tunic, which had a giant bite mark in it. "Does *this* answer your question?"

Okay, I needed to think. Mip wasn't listening to me, but she couldn't really help it. She was just a baby, after all. What would go through a baby's mind? She had been cooped up in her pen all morning, and now she wanted to play.

"Okay, Mip, let's play!"

She looked up at me and hopped. I hopped. She ran. I ran beside her all the way to the fresh stream that came down out of the mountain. She bent and drank. I dunked my face in the water. Mip bleated sweetly. I thought that was her way of laughing at me.

"You know what, Mip? You remind me of Tansy back home." I sighed. "I bet Grandpa is working in the rice field and Grandma is making new baskets. I'm sure Tansy is eating them faster than she can weave them."

All of a sudden I thought maybe it wouldn't be so bad if I failed the first test. At least then I'd get to go back home to the people I loved.

But then Mip worked her soft nose into my hand. I stroked her ears. They were even more velvety than Tansy's. If I became a Guardian, my job would be to protect creatures just like Mip. I liked the idea of doing something so important.

I scooped my fingers into the bowl, covering them with green paste. "Now, if you want to play tomorrow, you have to take your medicine today, okay?" I let Mip lick the medicine off my fingers.

"Good girl!" I said. "Now, was that so bad?"

Brother Chalad clapped as I led Mip back into the pen. "Astonishing, Plum! I'm very impressed."

"Really?"

He nodded. "Just see how the others are doing."

My classmates were covered in green goo. They had scooped their lambs up in their arms and were dragging them back to the corral, kicking and bleating. Cherry had medicine caked in her hair. "Plum, you put your lamb in a headlock, didn't you?"

I laughed. I felt pretty proud of myself.

But then I heard Rella say in a loud voice, "I'm not surprised Plum did so well. She probably lived in a sheep pen. At least, that's what she smells like."

Some of the Nakhon Island kids snickered. All my pride evaporated, and my face burned hot. I was glad Brother Chalad was there, because otherwise I would have tripped Rella and pushed her down into the mud.

In Hand class, Master Dew had a surprise for us too. After weeks of escape drills, conditioning, and doing everything *but* fighting, we were finally paired up to start sparring.

Cherry couldn't contain herself. She was bouncing so much I thought she was going to levitate. "I'm *so* ready to fight!"

Master Dew smiled. "All right, Cherry. You get your wish. Come and attack me."

Cherry looked shocked, like Master Dew had just given her a giant birthday cake. Then she got a fierce glimmer in her eye and rushed headlong at Master Dew.

Cherry had been wrestling and fighting way longer than any of us. If anyone was a match for Master Dew, it was her.

She threw herself into attacking our teacher. But Master Dew blocked every one of Cherry's moves with speed and ease. And then, just when it seemed like Cherry was finally going to get in a kick, Master Dew grabbed her ankle and used it to flip Cherry onto the ground.

Cherry looked up, her face filthy with dust, and grinned bigger than I'd ever seen. "That was awesome! You've got to teach me how to do that!"

Master Dew laughed as she helped Cherry to her feet. "There is a joy in your energy that we could all learn from. All right, let's partner up!"

Master Dew led us through some simple sparring drills: blocking kicks and punches from our partners. I was worried Cherry would overpower me, but I was surprised to find that I could actually block her attacks.

Now I understood why Master Dew had made us practice escapes so much. During every match, we ended up on the ground at some point. When that happened, if we couldn't escape from underneath our partners, it was all over.

I also understood why we had spent weeks building up our endurance. Sparring with another person was exhausting.

We continued the drills, changing partners each time until we had been matched up with everyone in the class. I was sweaty and spent by the time I got matched up with

Rella. She was sweating too, but she grinned like she was ready to eat me up.

"Come on, pig farmer," she said with a sneer. "Pretend I'm a big bucket of slop you can't wait to roll in."

I seethed with anger and rushed full force at her.

At the last moment, she stepped aside and shoved me to the ground. I pushed myself up, but before I could attack, Rella hooked her toes behind my ankle and swung me to the ground again, onto my back.

It knocked the wind out of me, and I rolled onto my side, heaving. Then I bolted up and got into a fighting stance. We were supposed to be taking it easy, but Rella rushed at me and started throwing full punches. *Block! Block! Block! Ha, take that, Rella!*

I could feel my anger toward her surging through my body. I swung my leg around and brought my heel down hard to whack her in the shoulder.

Before I could make contact, a hand caught my foot. I looked up. It was Master Dew. She tipped my leg up until I fell backward onto the ground again.

I groaned as I slowly sat up.

"Girls," she said in a scolding tone, "that wasn't the assignment. Apparently you have so much energy that you need to jog up to the Sunrise Temple to get it all out."

I was out of breath already. But I bowed to Master Dew and headed for the temple stairs.

Halfway up the steps, I turned to see how close Rella was. But she wasn't there. She must have run off and not taken her punishment.

I should have known she'd cheat in every way.

CHAPTER 17

I had never been so glad that Rella had started skipping Breath class. Master Sunback's lessons might have been boring, but at least I didn't have to deal with a cruel classmate.

"You are only the breath, in and out. Only the breath . . ." repeated Master Sunback.

My mind was still fixated on Rella, and when I breathed out, a frustrated sigh fluttered from my lips. I quickly shut my mouth before Master Sunback could hear.

Too late. "My dear Trainees," she said. "We will stop our lesson for a moment. I can feel that you are like guitars with the strings stretched too tight. Let me answer your questions, and let's see if we can ease the tension." She turned to me and smiled. "Plum, let's start with you. You have a question for me?"

I cleared my throat. "Well, Master Sunback, I wonder if maybe some of us were never meant to be very good at Breath. Like, maybe we're Heart Guardians."

"Or Hand!" blurted Cherry.

Some of the other kids murmured and nodded in agreement, and I was very glad I wasn't the only one wondering what the point of this class was.

Master Sunback nodded. "I see. You think that if you are not a Breath Guardian, you don't need to learn the power of the breath. But do any of you question the need to learn defense in your Hand class?"

"Well, that's different," said Mikko. "Everyone has to know how to defend themself."

"And everyone should learn some Heart skills," said Salan, "in case they have to help a creature who's hurt."

"Ah, but you don't think you need to breathe?" asked Master Sunback with a tilt of her chin. "The Great Beast gave us three gifts for a reason. Without mastering Breath, you will not be able to access your Guardian powers."

Mikko threw his hands up. "Master Sunback, it sure

would help if we knew what our powers were going to be! I mean, what are we working so hard for?"

Master Sunback tilted her head one way and then the other. And then she transformed.

We all gasped and scooted back. Master Sunback was a bearded lizard with sunset-red scales. When she stood on her back legs, she was as tall as Mikko. She peered at him with her dark eyes and beckoned for him to stand beside her.

Mikko gulped and went to the front of the class.

Master Sunback put one scaly claw on Mikko's shoulder. "My own powers are in recognizing the strengths of others." She winked. "A century of being a teacher helps too."

A century? How old *was* Master Sunback, anyway?

"Mikko, please shut your eyes."

Mikko smashed his eyelids closed.

"Let's breathe together, just like we do in class," said Master Sunback.

For a few minutes we watched as Mikko stood with his eyes shut, breathing in and out. Then Master Sunback tapped him, and they both opened their eyes.

"Mikko, your abilities are in stamina and endurance. If you pass the first test, I can almost guarantee that you will be a Hand Guardian."

Mikko's whole face glowed. "Thank you, Master Sunback! I'll work so hard, and I *will* pass!"

Master Sunback smiled. "Now, who would like to go next?"

A dozen hands shot up into the air. Master Sunback selected Salan and, just like she had done with Mikko, placed her claw on his shoulder. After a few minutes of breathing, she said, "Salan, you pay attention to all the little details. That's important in detecting disease and illness." Master Sunback winked at him. "Good qualities for a Heart guardian to have."

Salan grinned, and we all clapped for him.

Master Sunback wagged a scaly claw at all of us. "Now, for these predictions to become realities, you must all attend to your studies. These powers will only be realized if you are able to transform into Guardians."

Next, Master Sunback called on Hetty. Her strength was in sensing danger, a classic Breath Guardian skill. Twist and Sam were also on track to become Breath Guardians—Twist was skilled at sensing changes in the weather, and Sam just had super senses in general.

No surprise, Cherry's strength and tenacity also made her a likely Hand Guardian. So was Basil, who was quick and good at escaping. Basil's twin, Drum, was in the Heart Guardian group, along with gentle Emmie.

I watched all of them and clapped along as Master Sunback told them their abilities. I shook my head as I thought of Rella, missing this most incredible day of class.

Finally, the moment I had been waiting for arrived.

"Plum, it's your turn, my dear."

I wiped my sweaty fingers on my tunic as I stood up in front of Master Sunback. I took a deep breath and shut my eyes, wondering what my strengths could be.

I'm probably a Heart Guardian. Ooh, but what if I'm Hand? Chill out, Plum, and just be happy with whatever you get.

"Plum, focus only on breathing," whispered Master Sunback. "You must let everything else in your mind go. Try again."

I nodded and took another deep breath. I felt Master Sunback's scaly grip on my shoulder loosen. When I opened my eyes, her pleased smile had changed into a look of curiosity. Her blue tongue flicked in and out as she peered at my face.

I swallowed hard. Why was she looking at me like that?

From the direction of the kitchen, we heard the lunch bells ring out. "Ah!" said Master Sunback. "Lunchtime already. Let's stop there for today, shall we?" She transformed back into human form and clapped her hands. "You mustn't miss the most important part of the day!"

The other trainees chatted excitedly as they gathered up their shoes and bags.

I followed after them, casting one last look at Master Sunback. The old woman stared at the ground, tapping her chin. Whatever she had seen in me had left her confused.

She wasn't the only one.

I had to wait two days to speak with Master Sunback again. She was called away on some Guardian business, and Master Dew took over Breath class in her absence. It wasn't until Saturday—our rare day off from classes and chores—that I got my opportunity.

I found her on the Lotus Court, kneeling beside one of the lotus ponds, dressed in her muddy work clothes. Her face was tilted up, like she was drinking in the sunlight. I dropped into a bow.

"Master Sunback? Can I talk to you?"

She held a pair of tweezers out to me. "Perfect timing, Plum," she said with a smile. "I need to do an extremely boring job, and now you can help me."

Master Sunback pushed the tweezers into my hands as I knelt on the stones beside her. She showed me how to use them to pluck out the duckweed that grew in thick green mats among the flowers. As I worked, she tenderly cupped a pale lotus blossom in her hand.

"I baby these plants, but the truth is, they are very tough. Did you know that lotus seeds can be dried out for a thousand years and still sprout when they are planted in the mud?"

"Really?"

"Oh yes, such a magnificent plant." She smiled at me as I plucked the weeds. "You are very good with plants, Plum."

"Thank you, ma'am."

"And you are good with animals," she added.

"Thank you, ma'am."

"The other teachers tell me that you work hard and that you are an excellent student."

I started to blush. "Well, thank you, I try to—"

"So how come you don't listen in my class?"

I sat up on my heels. "That's not true! I pay attention to every word you say!"

She shook her head and pointed a finger at me. "No. You hear my words, but you don't follow them. Your body is breathing, but you let your mind run around like a racehorse. I can see it."

"You can?" I frowned. "Master Sunback, is this why you looked at me so funny in our last class? Because I didn't listen?"

"No . . . that's not the reason."

I turned the tweezers over and over in my hands. "Is it because I'm not actually Guardian material? Is it because you made a mistake in bringing me here?"

She sat back and put her hand on my knee. "Plum, I do *not* make mistakes regarding my Trainees. You were selected to come to Lotus Island because you are very special."

"That's what my grandparents tell me too. But maybe I'm just *different*." I looked in the direction of the beach, where the other Trainees had gone to swim. "I'm not like all the other kids here. They've known all their lives that they wanted to be Guardians."

"Plum, do *you* want to be a Guardian?"

I felt like the answer to that question was darting around in my brain like a twile-fly.

"I want . . . I want to figure out who I'm supposed to be," I said. "And I definitely don't want to fail the first test. I don't want to go home a failure."

She tilted her face to the side. "Who told you that going home would be a failure? It's not something I have ever said."

"No, but—"

"There are some people who come to Lotus Island who are not meant to be Guardians. When they leave here, they discover different paths. That's a good thing."

"Yes, but—"

"And don't dwell too much on what happened in our last class," Master Sunback interrupted. "Just because I couldn't easily place you doesn't mean you won't become a Guardian."

She went back to tending the lotus. "Plum, if you are meant to be a Guardian, then your Guardian form is already inside you, waiting. There is no shortcut to becoming what you already are. Don't try to be powerful, be strong, be magical. You cannot be a Guardian—you cannot be *anything*—if you cannot just *be*."

I shut my eyes and shook my head. "I'm not sure I understand."

She patted my knee. Her hand was warm from the sun. "Follow what I have taught you in Breath class. Don't dismiss it as simple or foolish. It's not easy, I know. But I believe that you can do it."

I opened my eyes. It meant a lot that Master Sunback believed in me. I only wished that I could believe too.

CHAPTER 19

That night I lay in bed, thinking about the things Master Sunback had told me. I could hear Cherry snoring softly on her mat. I opened my eyes. The moon was more than half full, a reminder of how close we were to our first test.

Suddenly I saw Rella sit up in bed. I shut my eyes tight, then peeled one eyelid open so I could see what she was doing. She was silent as a shadow as she swung her legs off her mat, slipped on her shoes, and tiptoed out the door.

I lay in bed for a few more moments before going to the window. Sure enough, there was Rella, tiptoeing down the moonlit path below and into the forest. What could she be up to?

I slipped a robe over my shoulders and put my shoes on.

I climbed down the cobra grapevine and followed after her. My heart pounded. What would I say if she caught me?

I hadn't gone far when I heard something in the bushes beside me.

"Who's there?" I hissed.

A small white thing burst out of the vegetation. It looked at me and bleated.

I exhaled with relief. "Oh, Mip! You scared me! But what in the world are you doing out of your pen?"

I knelt down and held out my arms. Mip began trotting toward me and then froze. She looked up into the dark trees behind me and sniffed the air.

"It's all right, girl. Come on, I'll get you back where you belong."

Mip's little legs began to tremble. I reached out to scoop her up in my arms, but she let out a frightened bleat and took off running in the other direction.

"Mip, come back!"

I hesitated, torn between my desire to help the little lamb and my burning curiosity about what Rella was doing. But I couldn't let Mip run wild. There were too many places on the island where she could get hurt.

I took off after Mip, all the way to the Lotus Court and around the back of the kitchen building. I followed the sound of her frightened bleats as my feet padded over the soft earth near the garden.

"Mip? Are you there? I'm here to help!"

I heard a rustle in the orchard by the garden. I looked up to see a large dark shape emerge from the trees. It was some sort of enormous animal. As it approached, I realized it was a wolfhund—the biggest dog I had ever seen, with a lean snout like a wolf's and a coat of sable-brown fur. Was this a Guardian? But who could it be? And why wasn't it speaking? The beast nodded in the direction Mip had run, then bowed to me, dropping to its knees.

I understood that the wolfhund wanted to give me a ride. Even though I was afraid, there was no time to waste if I was going to save Mip. I climbed on, and the great dog took off, loping across the meadow.

But where should we go? Mip could be anywhere.

The sound of fluttering wings filled the air. I imagined I could hear the bats and moths whispering to one another: *Have you seen her? Have you seen the little lamb? Have you, have you?*

Suddenly a thousand golden pinpricks of light sparkled in the black night. Twile-flies! They were flashing in a pattern, pointing toward the eastern side of the island.

"That way," I told the wolfhund. "Follow the lights!"

I held tight to the scruff of fur on the dog's neck as it bounded over the grass. As we neared the eastern cliffs, I saw Mip ahead of us.

"Mip! Don't get close to the edge!"

The wolfhund slowed, then stopped so I could climb down.

Mip must have been so scared, because she skittered even closer to the cliff. Fortunately a spindly laurel bush stood between her and the cliff's edge. I took a deep breath and slowly approached her.

"It's all right, Mip," I said, inching closer to her. "No one is going to hurt you." I whispered to the laurel bush, "Don't let her fall, Sister Laurel."

The branches of the laurel bush seemed to fold protectively around Mip, holding her still and calming her down. I reached for her and tucked her securely under one arm. But just as I was sure we were both safe, I felt the rocks beneath us crumble and give way. We started to fall. I clutched Mip tight and shut my eyes.

As my body fell through the air, I felt a hand encircle my wrist and grab tight.

"I've got you!" shouted a voice above me.

I opened my eyes. Far beneath me, the moonlight reflected on the waves. I looked up to see who had saved Mip and me from plunging into the ocean below.

"What the . . ." I whispered. "*Sam?*"

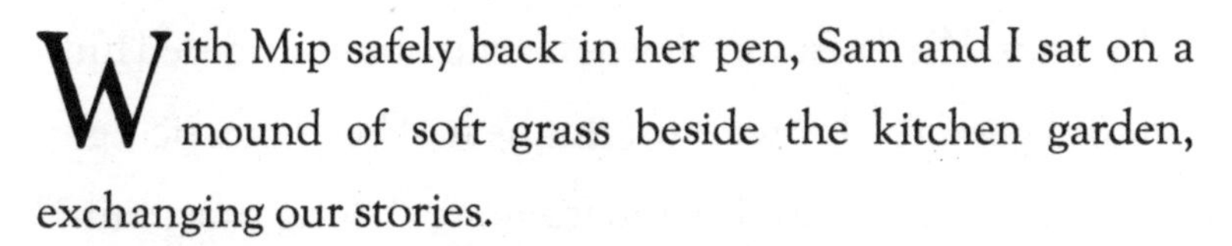

CHAPTER 20

With Mip safely back in her pen, Sam and I sat on a mound of soft grass beside the kitchen garden, exchanging our stories.

"So I was in the bample orchard practicing transforming and, well, this is going to sound weird," said Sam bashfully, "but I could *smell* you. Not that you smell bad! I could hear you too. I think it's part of my Guardian powers. When I'm a wolfhund, my senses are dialed all the way up."

I leaned back and looked at him, still amazed by what he had done. "How long have you known how to transform?"

"A couple of days now. I didn't want anyone else to know, so I've been practicing late at night when everyone's asleep."

"But why not tell anyone?" I asked.

Sam pushed his glasses up onto his nose. "I didn't want the other kids to know I'd learned so early. They already hate me. I'm sure they'd think my mother had arranged some special favors for me or something."

I frowned. He was right. And as much as I hated to admit it, I would have thought the same thing.

"I've been meditating since I was really little," Sam continued, "and I practice every chance I get, even when we have free time. One day it all just clicked. I looked down and I had . . . paws."

I thought of how I never saw Sam hanging out with the other kids. I had assumed it was because he considered himself too good to play with us. But he had been practicing!

"You've wanted to be a Guardian for a long time, huh?" I asked him.

He nodded. "It's been my dream forever. It felt so good to work together to save Mip tonight. Imagine doing that all the time. What could be better?"

I smiled. "It did feel really good to help her."

"My mom wasn't sure I should come here," said Sam. "I think she was afraid I would fail. But now I can't wait to tell her what I can do!"

Sam looked proud of himself. Not in a smug way, like

Rella, but like someone who'd been working really hard at something that had finally paid off.

"You're looking at me funny," he said. "Did I say something wrong? Sorry." He sighed and looked down at the grass. "I haven't hung out with other kids much."

I shook my head. "Actually, I'm the one who owes you an apology. This whole time I had you all wrong. I thought you were spoiled."

"It's okay," said Sam. "I probably am spoiled and don't even know it. I don't *want* to be, but I haven't had the most normal life. It's part of why I wanted to come to Lotus Island. I wanted to know what it was like to be around normal kids." He looked at me and grinned. "I did ask the teachers for one favor, though."

"You did?"

"I asked them to keep us on garden duty and not make us rotate."

I gasped. "That was you!"

He chuckled. "I saw how much you liked it, and I told them, 'If you want to grow twice as many vegetables, let Plum stay on garden duty. She sings to the eggplant.' "

"I do not!"

Sam raised his eyebrows.

"Okay, fine, I sing for them!" I said. "They like smooth melodies, okay?"

That made him laugh.

"I thought you thought I was some dirty farm girl," I said.

"What? No! I think what you can do is amazing. You're so good in the garden, and you're the only one who can get the dough lambs to do anything."

I shrugged. "I've always been good with animals."

"It's not just that. Plum, I heard you talk to that laurel bush tonight, and it actually *listened* to you."

I laughed. "You were imagining that!"

"I saw the bush wrap its branches around Mip," said Sam, "after you told it to."

The strange thing was that I had seen it too. I thought about the old yamyam tree that had shown me the path into the forest and the vines that had seemed to move out of my way. Was Sam right? Did those plants actually *understand* what I was saying?

I rubbed my shell pendant and shook my head. "What we saw was probably just a trick of the light. If I could get plants and animals to listen to me, I'd give a lot more orders."

Sam made a face like he wasn't entirely convinced. He pointed to my necklace. "And how about that shell? Did you talk a snail into giving it to you?"

I smiled and held it out toward him. "My mom left it for me before she died. My grandma said she put her dreams for me into it."

"Oh, you mean a dream amulet," said Sam.

I shook my head, confused. "I don't know what you're talking about."

Sam reached inside his shirt collar and pulled out a gold charm with a ruby jewel set into it. "A dream amulet. It's an old tradition on Nakhon Island. Parents whisper their dreams for their children into a charm or a stone and give it to them for luck. Here, listen."

Sam cupped his hands around the gold charm and blew a warm breath onto it. When he opened his hands, a soft light, like a tiny ball of starlight, glowed from the ruby gem. He held the charm up to my ear.

I heard the faintest echoing whisper of a woman's voice: "Wealth and power will flow to you like water from a rain."

"Sam, that's amazing. Whose voice is that?"

Sam let the pendant dangle again on its chain. "My mother's. Her dream was for me to be rich and powerful. We already are, so I guess that was kind of a waste."

I laughed. "Well, your necklace is *gold*. Mine is just a plain shell. I'm pretty sure it's not a dream amulet or anything fancy like that."

He shrugged. “Ask a hermit crab which necklace is more valuable. It’d pick your shell for sure.”

I squeezed my necklace tight. The sun was starting to come up. We needed to head back to our rooms before the teachers were up.

I walked him back to his private dorm.

“See you during chores,” Sam called as I continued on to my own dorm. “Maybe you can teach me your eggplant song.”

“Just wait till you hear what I sing for the pumpkins!”

I smiled as I walked up the steps to my room. There was still so much I felt unsure about. But one thing was certain: I felt less alone than I had before.

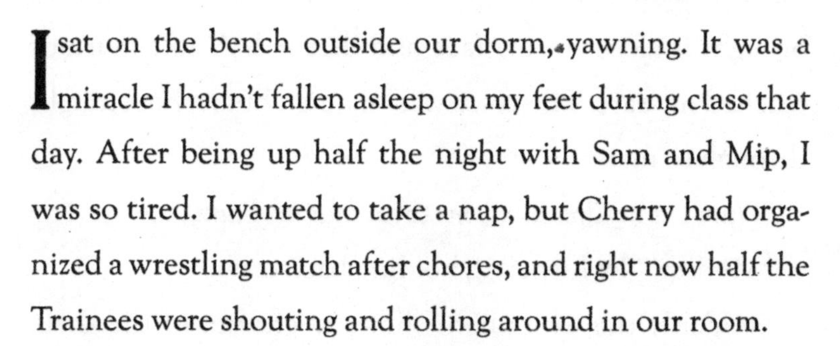

CHAPTER 21

I sat on the bench outside our dorm, yawning. It was a miracle I hadn't fallen asleep on my feet during class that day. After being up half the night with Sam and Mip, I was so tired. I wanted to take a nap, but Cherry had organized a wrestling match after chores, and right now half the Trainees were shouting and rolling around in our room.

Rella was with them. I had kept an eye on her all day, but she'd avoided meeting my gaze. Something was up, but I knew that if I asked her about it, she would just make some joke and wave me off. I'd have to catch her in the act if I wanted the truth.

I swung my legs beneath the bench and tapped my finger against my shell necklace. I smiled. It was funny to think that Sam had suggested it was a dream amulet. As if my humble little shell were anything like his gold necklace from fancy Nakhon Island.

Hold on. I suddenly remembered that my mother had been born on Nakhon Island. Could it be that she had made the same sort of necklace for me? My heart fluttered at the thought that I might be able to hear my mother's voice. I cupped my hands around the shell and blew a hot breath onto it.

At first nothing happened, and I felt silly for even trying. But then I saw it: a faint white glow inside the shell. I brought it closer to my face and listened. A soft murmur reached my ears. The voice was so quiet, but it shot straight through to me.

"*Plum . . . my dream . . . my dream for my Plum . . .*"

"Mother?" I whispered, holding back tears.

Suddenly the white light shot straight out of the shell. It hovered like a twile-fly right in front of my face. Its light pulsed like a heartbeat. I reached my hand timidly out to it. "Mother?" I whispered. "Is that your voice?"

The white light flitted away from my hand. I got to my feet, following it down the path toward the old forest.

"Mother! Wait!"

The light disappeared into the trees. I followed it as it

veered through the undergrowth. I stumbled over tree roots, not thinking about where I was going, not looking back. I didn't want to lose sight of the little light. But I had the feeling it didn't want to lose me either.

It wasn't until I was out of breath and sweating that I realized where we were going. The light stopped in the shadow of the ruined temple we had found on our first day on Lotus Island. It waited for me to catch my breath and then floated inside the temple.

I tiptoed after it as it traced the murals painted on the walls. I ran my fingers along the panels. I didn't know how to explain it, but I felt the presence of my mother as if she stood beside me.

"Why did you bring me here?" I whispered, not wanting to break the spell.

The light bobbed along the mural, illuminating the story of the Great Beast and the creation of the Santipap Islands. It blazed brighter as it traced a path to the creation of the Guardians—the Heart, the Hand, and the Breath. When the light reached the spot where the wall had crumbled, it hovered there, like it wanted to go farther, to show me more.

Tears choked my throat. "Mother! What is it?"

The light flared and darted away from my outstretched fingers toward the crumbling stones that covered up the

rest of the mural. I was worried it would disappear into a crack in the rocks and I would lose my mother's voice forever. I shot my hand out and closed my fingers around the light. The warmth of it spread all through my body. I took a deep breath. I had never felt so safe, so confident, so sure.

Slowly, I opened my fingers. The white light flickered faintly as it drifted up to my shell pendant and back inside.

I wiped my tears away and sank to my knees. I looked up at the mural, the gold paint gleaming faintly in the shadows. I couldn't believe it. I had been visited by my mother's spirit, and I had heard her voice.

My mother wanted me to become a Guardian. I just knew it.

I pressed my palms together at my chest and bowed my head.

"Mother," I whispered, "I promise you that I will make your wish come true."

I opened my eyes. I would become a Guardian. No matter what it took.

CHAPTER 22

From that moment on, I threw myself into my studies. We had only one week left until our first test. When we were told that we could take the next few days off from our chores, I took full advantage. While the other Trainees caught up on sleep or meditated, I used the time to run through our Hand drills over and over. When I was too tired to drill, I sat and imagined the way it would feel to fulfill my mother's dream. If my mind started to wander, I forced it to come back and concentrate on this one all-important goal.

After a couple of days, something didn't feel right. My fingers longed to dig into the dirt of the garden. I missed the smell of wet soil and green growing life. But I couldn't waste one moment on that stuff. I needed to focus.

"Trainees, with the first test just around the corner, it's time we talked about transformation," said Master Dew in Hand Class.

We all murmured excitedly. This was what we had been waiting for.

"Many Trainees find it helpful to have a specific movement that triggers their transformation. You can train your body to take on its Guardian form every time you perform that move. Let me show you mine."

Master Dew crouched low on one leg and held the other straight, like she was getting ready to pounce on something. She shut her eyes, then sprang forward with her hands out. But now her hands were paws, and she was covered in black jaicat fur.

Master Dew winked at us and then transformed back into her human self. "I want you to spend today's class listening to your bodies. Find your own moves."

Salan raised his hand. "How do we know what move we should use?"

Mikko stood with his arms at his sides, waggling his fingers. "I think this might be mine."

"Focus on your breath, and let it move through your body," said Master Dew. "The motion that's the one for you will feel *right*. When you find it, you'll know."

We spread out and got started. It felt a little silly to be waving my arms and legs around with my friends watching. When none of us could stop giggling, Master Dew had us close our eyes.

I tried squatting down like Master Dew. I swung my arms to one side, then the other. I stepped forward. I jumped up. *Concentrate, Plum.*

I peeled one eye open. The other kids were totally absorbed in the assignment. Everyone had their eyes closed, and they moved slowly, as if their bodies were covered in honey.

I watched Cherry take up a wide stance and pull one arm back like she was drawing the string of a bow. She did the motion again and again, then broke into a huge smile. "This is totally my move! It feels so right!"

Hetty balanced on one foot and swept the other foot in a wide arc in front of her. "When I do this, I can feel this shivery coolness all over!"

"Excellent, Hetty! That's a sign that you're on the right track." Master Dew turned to me. "How about you, Plum? Did you find a motion that feels right?"

I nodded and pretended to practice. Master Dew continued on to congratulate all the other Trainees around me who were connecting with their moves. She had said that when we found the right one, we would know. But the only thing I knew was that I had failed—again.

❧

"Dode beef efeff um," mumbled Cherry.

"What?"

Cherry swallowed the bite of fruit in her mouth and took a big drink of coconut water. We were sitting in the shade of a twisty rose apple tree after lunch.

"I said, don't beat yourself up. Not everyone figured it out."

"I was watching," I said. "Everyone did. Everyone but me."

"Well, there's your problem. You weren't supposed to have your eyes open!" Cherry set her hand on my shoulder. "It's like Master Sunback says: Our Guardian powers have always been with us. They're just beneath the surface. You can't force them out."

I squeezed her hand. Cherry was such a sweet friend, but she didn't understand. She was a natural Guardian. If I was going to pass the first test, I couldn't just sit back and hope for it to happen.

Master Dew came over to where we were all resting. To our surprise, she was followed by a bright yellow hoverbot. "Sam, you have a visitor. Your mother is waiting for you down at the dock."

Sam blushed as he followed the hoverbot to the dock.

Master Dew turned to the rest of us. "Little brothers and sisters, Brother Chalad has offered to take you on a hike to West Shore Falls this afternoon."

Everyone whooped and got up to change clothes. Hetty rolled her eyes in the direction of the dock. "Must be nice to be Sam. No one else is allowed to have visitors!"

"Yup, spoiled," said Cherry. "You coming, Plum?"

I frowned, feeling bad for Sam. It wasn't his fault his mom had broken the rules. I was glad for him. He missed his mother so much. Suddenly I had the overwhelming urge to hear my own mother's voice again.

"You go on, and I'll catch up," I said to Cherry.

I waited for her and Hetty to walk away, and then I turned in the other direction.

If I could just connect with my mother's spirit one more time, I knew it would give me the boost I needed to do well on the first test.

I raced toward the forest.

My feet flew along the path to the ruins. I had felt so sure that I could become a Guardian when I was here last. I just needed to tap into that feeling again.

I stopped when I reached the little pond with the lotus buds. Their white petals had started to unfold. I breathed in their soft scent as I knelt down in a beam of sunlight.

"I know you wanted me to be a Guardian, but I need help," I whispered to the pendant. "I'm trying so hard, but I just don't know how to do this."

I breathed into the shell, just like I had before, but this time there was no soft glow or sound of my mother's voice.

Suddenly I heard a noise in the bushes behind me.

"Who's there?" I whispered. I swore I caught a flash of fur, but then it was gone.

My heart thudded as I tiptoed away from the pond and into the trees. I hid behind a large broken stone statue and listened. Voices. And footsteps, coming closer.

With horror, I realized that one of the voices belonged to Master Sunback. I searched for an escape, but I couldn't go anywhere without them seeing me. I crouched lower and tried to be completely silent.

"My son is very quiet, I know," said a second voice. "If you could be easy with him, I would be very grateful."

I recognized that voice. It was the same one I had heard coming from Sam's pendant. Lady Ubon!

"My lady," said Master Sunback, "all our Trainees must do the work for themselves. That said, Sam is a wonderful student, and he is very talented. I don't think you need to worry about him."

I risked peeking around the edge of the statue. They made a strange pair: tall, elegant Lady Ubon and small Master Sunback in her simple robes.

"You make me a very proud mother," said Lady Ubon with a warm smile. "And now I will tell you the true reason for my visit. Last week a team of three Guardians on

Bidibop Island stopped a fleet of boats from Nakhon Island and made them turn back."

"Yes, they told me," said Master Sunback. "The coral reef near Bidibop Island is very fragile, and your fishermen were dropping anchor, destroying coral that had been growing for thousands of years. They were also overfishing, taking far too much in their nets."

"Those fishermen feed the people of Nakhon Island," said Lady Ubon. "I will speak with them about their anchors, of course, but this is not the first time your Guardians have gotten in our way. Please order them to allow us to fish there."

Master Sunback's voice prickled with irritation. "They are not *my* Guardians, and I do not give them orders, my lady. They have sworn an oath to protect life. I trust them to use their gifts to do so."

"I have a large population of people to protect," said Lady Ubon. "Their lives come first, surely."

"I have had this discussion with your family before," said Master Sunback with a sigh. "If you care for your people, you must care for the world they live in. Without the plants and animals of our islands, we humans will not last very long."

Now it was Lady Ubon's turn to sound annoyed. "Of course I care for the world we live in. In the years my family has ruled Nakhon Island, we have improved the lives of everyone there. We have banished disease. Everyone has the chance to own a home, to prosper and build a life for themselves. Which is much more than I can say for when the island was just a bunch of yamyam farmers."

"And what will you do when everyone on Nakhon wants a big fancy house?" said Master Sunback. "Where will they put them? And what will they build them with if you cut down all the trees? What will your people eat if you catch all the fish and run out of farmland?"

Lady Ubon's shoes clicked on the stones as she paced around the lotus pond, closer to me. I hardly dared to breathe.

"There is a solution, Master Sunback," she said.

Master Sunback spoke warily. "I have already given you my answer. Lotus Island is not for sale."

"Even you have to admit that the power of the Guardians is not what it once was," said Lady Ubon. "Does the Academy really need to take up one of the largest islands in Santipap?"

"It is true that with each passing year, the power of the

Guardians seems to fade a little more," said Master Sunback sadly. "But we are still needed."

"The Guardians will always be an important part of our history," said Lady Ubon kindly. "But we are heading into a new future, one of progress and prosperity. It may be time to step aside and let that new future unfold. I have told you that I will pay handsomely for this land."

Master Sunback's answer was so forceful it made me jump. "I would not sell you Lotus Island if you offered me every coin in Nakhon Island! The Guardians have sworn an oath to protect all the life throughout our islands. What future will there be if we abandon our duty?"

Lady Ubon was silent for a long time. Then she spoke calmly. "Master Sunback, I only want what is best for the people of Nakhon—for all Santipap. I will leave the matter alone for now, but this is something we cannot ignore for much longer. The day is waning, and I must get back to my duties in the city. I will find my son and bid him goodbye."

Their voices faded as they left, but I stayed still for a long time, thinking about everything I had heard. What had they meant about the power of the Guardians growing weaker? It was all so confusing.

I realized I had stayed too long, and the others would be wondering where I had gone. As I stood up, I was knocked to the ground, onto my back. I looked up and drew in a sharp breath.

I was staring into the fanged mouth of a giant leopard.

CHAPTER 24

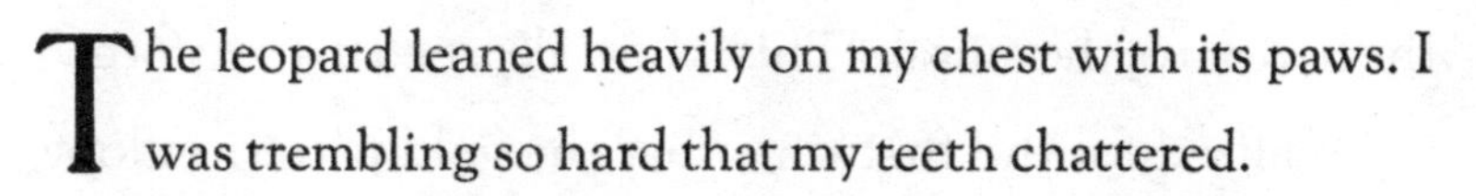

The leopard leaned heavily on my chest with its paws. I was trembling so hard that my teeth chattered.

But then Master Dew's training kicked in. Without even thinking, I popped my hips up to knock the leopard off balance. I used my advantage to curl my knees in and push out from underneath the beast. The next second I was on my feet and running.

I had gone only a few paces when I heard laughter behind me.

The laughter was taunting and cruel. And familiar.

Slowly I turned around. "Rella?" I whispered.

The leopard shifted like it was shrugging off its thick silvery coat. In its place stood Rella, cackling.

"Your face was priceless!" she said. "I've never seen someone so scared!"

I was too astonished by what I had just seen to be angry at her.

"You were the leopard? But how?"

"While you've been huffing and puffing in Breath class, I've been doing the real work of learning to transform."

"What do you mean?"

She walked toward the ruined temple and waved at me to follow her.

"This is where I come during class," she said, pointing to the bottom of the mural. "This is how I learned to transform."

I realized for the first time that the gold patterns along the bottom of the mural were actually words written in a looping, curling script.

"They're chants," whispered Rella. "Ancient magic from before the Santipap Islands even existed."

"What do they say?"

"I don't know exactly," said Rella. "They must be written in the language of the Old Home. But it doesn't matter. If you say them in the proper order, you can tap into that old magic." She smirked. "No breathing necessary."

"But why haven't our teachers said anything about this?" I asked. "If this is an easier way to transform, why not share it?"

"Because they don't want us to get so far so fast! They treat us like babies, making us do drills and chores. By using the ancient magic, you can access all the power right away. Watch."

She shut her eyes and placed her fingertips together. Then she began speaking in a low voice, repeating the same string of words over and over.

With a ripple of silver, she became the leopard again. She was massive, as tall as me even down on four paws. She stalked through the ruins like a trail of smoke. The shadows seemed to follow her and collect in pools around her paws. The air felt colder than it had a moment before.

"I'm just beginning to understand what being a Guardian really means," growled Rella. "This *power*—it's more than any of us realized."

She shook her feline head, and before my eyes, she vanished, melting into shadow.

"Rella?" I said, looking around for her. "Rella!"

She changed back into her human form, and the shadows scattered. She pointed to the mural. "You could learn all of this too, Plum. It took me a while to get the rhythm of the words, but once you have it, it's quite easy."

A strange, icy feeling crept up my back. "Why are you sharing this with me, Rella?" Even as I asked the question,

I knew the answer. "You want me to use the chants too so you're not the only one who could get in trouble." I folded my arms. "This isn't right, and you know it. You should stop."

A strange look flashed in her eyes: a mixture of loneliness and hunger. "Stop? And then what, Plum? Go home a nobody? I have to become a Guardian. I'm not like Sam Ubon. I don't have some shiny future laid out for me. If I want a good life, I have to fight for it any way I can."

I stared back at her. I had thought she was a fancy city kid with no worries. I was starting to realize that maybe I didn't know her at all.

Rella put her hand on my arm. "We could do this together. I could teach you. What does it matter how we transform as long as we can do it?" She tilted her head at me. "Unless those classes are working for you?"

My face must have given away my answer.

"Plum, are you seriously telling me you'd risk failing out of the Academy just because you won't learn some simple chants? I'm willing to share this with you as long as you don't tell anyone."

I sighed. "I won't tell your secret. But not because I want something from you. Because it's not my place."

She smiled. "Good. So will you use the chants?"

I cast my eyes down. "I don't know . . . I mean, no. I won't."

Rella shrugged and started walking away. "Well, if you change your mind, the words are right there. Your future is in your own hands," she called to me over her shoulder. "Think about it, Plum."

I stood still for a while before heading out. I cast one last look back at the mural. The late-afternoon sunlight hit the wall.

The gold-painted words of the ancient chant blazed like a fire.

Our last Breath class began much like the first.

"Breathe in . . . breathe out . . ." said Master Sunback. "I know many of you are nervous about the first test. But remember that our Guardian forms are always with us. We keep them buried with our many thoughts and worries. But when we focus on our breath and just being, we allow our truest selves to shine through."

As usual, breathing slowly made me feel calmer, which was a good thing after what had happened with Rella at the ruins. I hadn't told anyone else about the chants. Was that the right decision?

If Master Sunback could have read my mind, she would have told me not to hold on to those worries. She would have told me to let them float away like clouds moving across the sky. But I didn't want to do that. I wanted to focus on my problems. How else was I supposed to solve them?

"Excellent work today, Trainees," said Master Sunback when class was finished. "We are done, but you are welcome to sit here as long as you like. And remember that no matter what happens, no matter where you are in the world, you can always return to this place of peaceful stillness just by breathing."

I heard her get up and leave. My classmates stayed sitting, but I was ready to go. I was just about to stand up when I heard Cherry gasp. I opened my eyes and looked at her.

"Plum, are you seeing what I'm seeing?" she whispered.

Cherry's hands rested palms-up on her knees. Only they weren't hands anymore. They were furry paws with long claws.

Cherry flexed one paw, and the claws extended. The fuzzy skin between her fingers was webbed, like a duck's foot. "Oh my gosh!"

The other kids began to open their eyes. Their mouths fell open when they saw Cherry. Then everyone shut their eyes again. Their breathing sounded like a hurricane! It took a moment for calm to return.

I shut my eyes too. I tried to remain focused on myself, but peeking at everyone else was too tempting.

Salan suddenly had vibrant blue feathers covering his arms and neck. Twist's skin shimmered with rosy scales. One by one, all around me, my classmates began to show flickers of transformation. Some of them were only glimmers—a pop of fur here, a crest of feathers there. Others, like Cherry, were definitely in the middle of transforming. I half expected to look over and see her become a giant beast!

Sam sat very still, unchanged. I guessed that he didn't want to reveal that he could already fully transform into a wolfhund.

I shut my eyes and took a big breath to steady myself. I would *not* be the last one! I touched the shell pendant around my neck and focused on the thought of transformation. I was determined to do it through a sheer force of will.

But the next thing I knew, the lunch bells were ringing out. As the Trainees opened their eyes and stood up, their Guardian forms faded away. Everyone laughed and talked excitedly.

As for me? I hadn't managed a flicker of transformation. Not even one tiny patch of fur.

The gold letters of the chants gleamed in the shadows like they had been painted with embers. I took a deep breath and clutched the shell pendant tight in my fist. I had been worried that Rella would be at the ruins today, but to my relief, I was alone.

The first test was tomorrow. After my failure in Breath class, I knew this was my only hope of passing.

"Mother," I whispered, "I'm going to do this for you."

I waited to feel that wonderful warmth that had come from the shell before, but I must have been too nervous to feel anything. I let go of the shell and reached into my pocket for the piece of paper and pencil I had brought.

I knelt at the base of the mural and started copying down

the chants. They were written in our alphabet, but I didn't understand the words. Rella had said that their power would help me even if I didn't know what I was saying. I hoped she was right.

I wrote down everything carefully, but then I ran into a problem. The mural covered the entire length of the temple wall, but a portion of the wall was hidden by crumbled stones. The chant continued underneath the rubble, out of sight. I wanted to pull some of the stones away from the wall, but I worried that messing with the rocks was too dangerous.

I frowned down at my paper. If I was missing some of the chant, would its power work for me? Well, it had worked for Rella. I wrote down as much as I could.

I sat back on my heels, took a deep breath, and began to read the words out loud.

My tongue tripped over the strange sounds at first, but then I found a rhythm. The words came out in a breathy murmur, like someone talking in their sleep. When I finished, nothing happened. Had I done it right?

I tried again, and then again, more slowly. As I spoke, I began to feel a strange tingling in my fingertips.

Suddenly the entire temple flooded with light. The images on the mural burst into motion. They floated and swayed as if the paintings were alive. The tingling in my fingers surged into my arms and legs. I felt so strong, like I could run to the top of a mountain or leap over trees. Rella had been right.

This was power. Pure power. It scared me.

I clamped my mouth shut and pressed my hands tight together. The light vanished like a candle being blown out. I sat still for a long time, breathing heavily.

I realized that I must have been in the middle of transforming, but I had forgotten to look at myself and figure out what my Guardian form was. But I didn't want to say the chants again right now. I didn't know what was more frightening: the overwhelming feeling of power or the fact that I wanted to feel it again.

I folded the piece of paper and put it in my pocket.

CHAPTER 27

The evening of the first test had arrived.

As I got in line with the rest of the Trainees to head toward the Lotus Court, I kept my eyes on my feet. I felt an arm slip into the crook of my elbow. Cherry smiled at me.

"It's going to go great," she said.

I smiled back, even though I wasn't so sure.

We gathered in the Lotus Court, just like we had on the first night we arrived. The sky was a deep blue, and the full moon had just begun to rise over the edge of the sea.

Master Sunback stood in front of us between Brother Chalad and Master Dew. They all wore the crisp white robes reserved for special ceremonies.

Master Sunback raised her arms in greeting. "My dear

Trainees, you have all worked so hard and learned so much. We could not be prouder of you. This is the moment you have been working toward. I will call you one by one, and you will come forward and make your transformation—or not. Remember that no matter what happens, by the time the full moon sets, you will be who you are. Just as you have always been."

I heard a soft cough behind me. I turned. Rella raised one eyebrow at me. I turned back around, my stomach fluttering faster than twile-fly wings.

"Sam," Master Sunback called gently, "I would like you to go first."

Sam looked nervously at all of us. Then he squared his shoulders, stood, and walked to stand in front of Master Sunback. He shut his eyes and did his move: placing his hands together in a deep bow. Instantly, he became the wolfhund who had helped me save Mip. All around me, the others murmured in awe.

Master Sunback smiled at him. "Congratulations, Novice Sam." Sam threw his head back and let out a howl of joy.

We all laughed and clapped for him.

And so it began. One by one, I watched as my friends were called and they took their place in front of our teachers. They transformed into furry, scaly, or feathered beasts, both powerful and beautiful. Salan became a bright blue wybird with a scissored tail. Mikko changed into a gigantic field sloth. And Hetty became an indigo hare with long, slender ears.

"Cherry, it's your turn," said Master Sunback.

I squeezed Cherry's hand, and then she walked to the front of the court. She did the move I had seen her practice, drawing one arm back like she was shooting an arrow. With a long exhale, Cherry grew and grew and grew. Our jaws dropped open. Her Guardian form was even bigger than Mikko's! She was a butter-colored bear with thick fur. She flexed her clawed paws, revealing webs of skin between the fingers.

"Are. You. Kidding me?" She threw up her arms and shouted, "A gillybear! I'm a gillybear!"

We jumped to our feet and cheered!

As we resumed our seats, a wave of sadness rushed over me. I was so happy for Cherry. But I realized with a twist in my heart that if I didn't pass this test, I might never see her again.

Master Sunback continued to call Trainees to the front. Behind me, I heard Rella whispering the words of the chant over and over. I knew them well because I had memorized them myself.

When it was her turn, Rella effortlessly transformed into the slinking silver leopard.

I was the only Trainee left sitting. My heartbeat thumped in my ears so loudly that I nearly didn't hear Master Sunback call my name.

"Plum. It's your turn now, my dear."

I stood and walked slowly to the front of the court. I turned to face away from the others. It was now or never. I could whisper the chant and no one would know. The words were on the tip of my tongue.

"Plum?" said Master Sunback. "Whenever you are ready."

I could feel the whole Academy holding its breath, waiting.

I held my breath too. The words of the ancient chant pounded in my thoughts.

The weight of the shell pendant rested against my

collarbone. *What was your dream for me, Mother?* Something special, something great. I knew deep in my heart that she would have loved for me to be a Guardian.

But not like this.

I bowed my head.

"I'm sorry, Master Sunback," I whispered. "I . . . can't do it."

"Plum—" she started to say, but I didn't hear the rest.

I was running away from the Lotus Court, the twile-flies a blur of light in my tear-filled eyes.

CHAPTER 28

I lay on my mat, listening to Cherry snore. I knew I would miss everything about her, even this. While the other Novices had celebrated, Cherry had stayed with me. She hadn't tried to make it better, because she knew nothing *could* make it better.

I rolled over onto my back. There was no use in wondering if I had made the right decision. It was too late. I had failed, no matter what Master Sunback said. Now I would go back to Grandma and Grandpa with nothing to show for my time here. And then what? What would I become now?

I heard a soft tapping coming from downstairs. I sat up. It was still hours before dawn. I pulled on my robe and tiptoed down the stairs. When I opened the front door, I found Sam waiting there.

"Sam, don't try to—"

Before I could finish, he grabbed my wrist and pulled me out the door.

"What are you doing?" I asked. "Where are we going?"

"To the kitchen garden," he said, pulling me faster.

I sighed. "I don't want to see it. It will make me too sad to say goodbye."

"I'm not taking you there to say goodbye," said Sam. "I'm taking you there to transform."

"What? I can't! You saw me. It's over."

He pointed up. The full moon had arced through the sky and was now sinking toward the horizon. "It's not over yet. The moon hasn't set."

Sam led me all the way to the pepper patch. "Plum, if you try again and you can transform, we can tell Master Sunback, and you'll be able to stay."

I shook my head. "I can't, I—"

"Listen. I've seen you when you're working here. You're a different person. I can't explain it, I just know this is the place where you are really *you*."

"Transforming is harder than singing to eggplants."

Sam reached out to put his hand on my arm and then

pulled it back. "Please try. If you go, I . . . I'll be . . . well, just give it one more shot, all right?"

I nodded. I knew what it felt like to need a friend. "All right. I'll try."

He smiled and backed away to give me space.

I took a deep breath and shut my eyes. I tried to do what Master Sunback always said in her class and clear my mind, but my thoughts were humming like a hoverbot motor.

What would my mother want?

What do I want?

I don't want to leave my friends.

I do want to see my grandparents.

I want to become something wonderful.

I shook my head and took another deep breath. Why was it so hard to let my thoughts get out of my way?

I didn't know why, but I sank to my hands and knees, like I always did when I weeded garden beds. I felt the soft, moist soil beneath my fingers. I breathed in its damp, rich scent. It was the smell of life flowing back and forth between living things. Oh, it would be hard to say goodbye to this garden! But maybe the time had come. I listened to the breeze gently ruffle the leaves around me. I heard the crickets singing. Their song seemed to say *A beautiful night, beautiful night, such a beautiful night!*

I breathed in again and caught the faint whiff of blossoms all the way from the Lotus Court. Those same old worrying thoughts tried to sneak into my head, but they felt less important now. I pushed them away and imagined them vanishing like mist clearing on a warm day.

Breathe.

There is nothing but the soil beneath my hands.

The crickets in the wood.

Their song in the night.

My breath in my body.

I wasn't sure how long I knelt in the dirt like that.

Finally, it was time. If I had to leave Lotus Island, I was ready.

"I'm sorry, Sam," I called out. "I tried, but I just couldn't—"

My eyelids fluttered open. Sam stood there grinning at me.

"What?" I asked.

And then I looked down at my hands.

No. Not hands.

Hooves.

CHAPTER 29

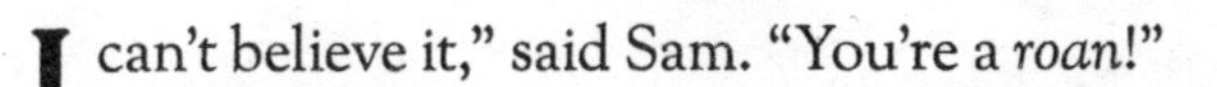

I can't believe it," said Sam. "You're a *roan*!"

"What the heck is a roan?" I stamped my hooves and whipped my head back and forth, trying to look at my body. No one had mentioned that when you transformed, it was really hard to tell what you had transformed into.

Sam laughed at me and led me to the garden shed. The sun had come up, bright enough that I could just make out my reflection in the window glass. Apparently a roan was a tall, deerlike creature with strong legs and a strawberry-brown coat. I dipped my head, swaying my slender red antlers back and forth. I didn't feel that uncontrollable surge of power I had felt when I'd spoken the chants. I just felt like . . . me.

“Roans are super-ancient animals,” said Sam. “I’ve only seen pictures of them in books.”

“A roan,” I whispered. And then I laughed. “I can’t believe it! I did it!”

“I knew you could do it! And just in time too.” Sam pointed to the horizon, where the full moon was sinking fast. “Let’s go find Master Sunback!”

With a bow of his head, he transformed into his wolfhund form and took off running across the grass toward the Lotus Court. I loped after him, slowly at first to get the hang of my new form. I only tripped twice—not bad for my first time on four legs.

And then I was galloping. I had never moved so fast! I caught up to Sam, then passed him. We ran and ran, my hooves flying across the grass, the wind in my antlers, the world whizzing by in a green blur.

Sam and I slowed as we crossed the empty Lotus Court, searching for Master Sunback, but it was still so early. No one was awake.

"Down there, on the beach!" called Sam. "I see someone!"

I trotted after him down the steps to the shore. Together we galloped across the wet sand, letting the ocean spray fly up behind us. At the far end of the beach sat an enormous gold-red lizard. As we approached, she shifted and shrank and became . . .

"Master Sunback!" I called, slowing to a walk.

"Ah, Plum," she said with a smile. "I always knew you would figure it out." She winked at Sam. "Looks like I'm not the only one who believed in you."

Sam and I both gave ourselves a little shake, releasing our Guardian forms, and bowed to our teacher.

"It was like you said, Master Sunback," I told her. "I just had to get out of my own way. And now every one of us has passed and become a Novice!"

Master Sunback's smile faded. "Not everyone, unfortunately. I had to speak privately with Rella. I tried to advise her many times before the test, but she went against everything I told her. She relied on shortcuts for her transformation, and I'm afraid I cannot let her stay."

Gosh, as much as I didn't get along with Rella, I didn't want this for her. I knew she would be devastated.

"My hope is that in time, Rella will find her place in the world," said Master Sunback. "Each of us needs that." She rested her hands on our shoulders. "Today I am happy. The Guardian Academy has a wonderful new class of Novices. Our islands are at peace. And the cooks have made sweet taro porridge for breakfast. Go, run, and be happy too!"

Sam and I took one look at each other. We didn't need to be told twice. We transformed back into our Guardian forms and took off racing up the beach.

The sun rose higher behind us, washing all of Lotus Island in golden beams of light.

CHAPTER 30

The next day I waited with the others on the beach and watched the small blue mail boat pull up to the dock.

"Our first batch of mail from our families," said Cherry, hopping from one foot to the other. "I'm so excited!"

Salan held a thick envelope. "I'm even more excited to mail this letter home and tell them that I'm a Novice!"

I smiled down at my own letter. I wondered how my grandparents would react to the news. I wished I could be there when they read it. The only sad thing about becoming a Novice was that I would have to wait longer before I had the chance to go home and visit them.

The next step in our Guardian training would be to learn how to control and magnify our powers so that one day we could use them out in the world. We would continue to learn about meditation, defense, and healing. But we would also start to focus on one element depending on what type of Guardian we were.

All the other kids had been easily labeled as Heart, Hand, or Breath Guardians. But it wasn't so obvious where I should fit. Our teachers had held a special meeting and decided that since I was so good with plants, I should study Heart with Brother Chalad. It bothered me that once again, I wasn't like everyone else. But I was happy to be a Heart Guardian and ready to dive into my studies.

The mail boat docked, and the captain started handing out the mail. I saw Rella standing alone and reading a letter.

The mail boat would be taking her back to Nakhon Island. She had stayed very quiet the past day and hadn't even said goodbye to Hetty or Cherry when she'd packed up her things in our room. She had been so mean to me, and I definitely didn't think I could call her a friend. But I also felt sad for her.

"Rella?" I said, jogging up to her. "Hey, I just wanted to see if you were okay."

She looked up from the letter she was reading, and her usual catlike smile returned. "Better than okay, actually." She held the letter out to me.

Dear Rella,

I have been informed that you failed the first test to become a Novice. I would like to extend an invitation for you to come and work with our team in the Office of National Prosperity in Nakhon Island. Bright young talents such as you are always welcome here.

Sincerely,
Lady Ubon

I handed the letter back to Rella. "Are you going to accept?"

She snatched the paper from my hand. "An invitation to work with the wealthiest family in all the islands? Of course I'm accepting it! Only a farm girl like you would ask such a question."

Even though it was nice of Lady Ubon to give Rella the opportunity, something about it also seemed strange to me. I wondered whether Sam or Master Sunback knew about the offer.

But I smiled at Rella and held out my hand to her. "I'm happy for you, Rella. Good luck, and take care of yourself."

She looked down at my fingers, and I thought maybe she would walk away. Instead she shook my hand. "Thanks, Plum. You too."

While she boarded the boat, I ran back to where Sam and Cherry stood talking. The mail boat captain came back with packages for both of them and a thick envelope for me. "Oh! It's a letter from my grandparents!" I sniffed the paper; it smelled just like our kitchen (and a little like goat breath).

Grandma and Grandpa wrote that they were both doing well, and they gave me a full account of the garden and Tansy. They missed me, but they were happy knowing I was doing something new and exciting.

I reached into the envelope and pulled out a paper packet. "Chai-melon seeds!" I exclaimed. "Yes! Just you wait—these are the best!"

"Well, what are we waiting for?" said Sam. "Let's go plant them!"

"Seriously," said Cherry. "I want some chai-melon ice cream as soon as possible!"

In the garden, my friends laughed and joked behind me as I knelt in the beds. I gave my shell pendant a little squeeze. Then I gently ran my fingers through the damp, dark soil until I found a pair of wriggling red worms.

"Hey, friends," I whispered to them. "Will you show me the best place for these melons?"

The worms pointed me to a nice open patch at the end of the bed, where I planted the seeds.

If there was one thing I'd learned, it was that the worms were usually right.

LEGENDS OF LOTUS ISLAND

INTO THE SHADOW MIST

Plum and her friends are traveling to misty Bokati Island. There, they will study with the mysterious Guardian Master Em, who is the keeper of the ancient Bokati forest there. The field trip comes just in time for Plum, who still can't figure out why she's so different from the other Novices on Lotus Island.

At first, Plum doesn't know what to make of this quiet and sometimes gloomy place. But it doesn't take long to discover that Bokati island is brimming with an incredible array of fascinating animals and plants.

When an unseen force begins to destroy the trees, putting the entire ecosystem at risk, Plum and her classmates must spring into action. Plum is determined to help, even though she's hiding secrets about her own Guardian powers from even her closest friends.

ABOUT THE AUTHOR

Christina Soontornvat is the bestselling author of two Newbery Honor books, *A Wish in the Dark* and *All Thirteen: The Incredible Cave Rescue of the Thai Boys' Soccer Team.* She is also the author of Scholastic's beloved fantasy series Diary of an Ice Princess, as well as the picture books *The Ramble Shamble Children* and *To Change a Planet.* As a child, Christina spent most of her time at her parents' Thai restaurant with her nose stuck in a book. These days, she loves nothing better than spending a day hiking and swimming in the creeks and swimming holes around Austin, Texas with her husband and two daughters. You can learn more about her work at soontornvat.com.